Reuniting with Her Prince

An Aldonia Royals Novel

Kristine Lynn

Reuniting with Her Prince
An Aldonia Royals Novel #3
Copyright © 2022 Kristine Lynn
All rights reserved.

ISBN (ebook) 978-1-958136-11-9
(print) 978-1-958136-12-6

Inkspell Publishing
207 Moonglow Circle #101
Murrells Inlet, SC 29576

Cover art by: Fantasia Frog Designs
Edited by: Audrey Bobek

To Erica and Stacy, my romance sisters. From Hallmark bingo to dreaming up love stories, to chasing our own—you two are my version of cozy Christmas flannels and hot cocoa by a fire with young, hot Santa.

KRISTINE LYNN

PROLOGUE: TWO YEARS EARLIER

I'm taking him home with me tonight.

It was Lissa's first thought when she laid eyes on the stranger across the teak wood bar. Her second thought wasn't quite so innocent. As if to punctuate her desire, a loud clap of thunder boomed, and the air vibrated within the small space. A storm was imminent in more ways than one.

He mimed a shiver and smiled back at her—totally not innocent, either—then nodded toward a table by the entrance, his grin an eager invitation.

"Nope," she mouthed, curling her finger in an invitation of her own. *Come here.*

He smiled and shrugged then started toward her, his saunter promising fun. And in the nick of time, too. Had it really been almost a full month since she'd left everything behind and bought a ticket to the one place no one would recognize her?

One month. Too short a time to forget the hell awaiting her back home, but an infinity to live without satisfying certain… *needs.* Needs that, thanks to her parents and their helicoptering, she'd ignored too long.

Her cell buzzed on the hardwood bar top. *Crap.* Her

mother. Again.

It figured, didn't it? Her mother always did have an eerie ability to interfere in her life, particularly when things were about to get good. Interfering only to ruin them, of course.

"Get you something else?" the bartender asked.

"No, thanks. I'm waiting for someone." Someone tall, dark, and handsome and only half a bar from her.

Which meant she definitely did not have time for her mother, father, or anyone not drinking martinis on the beach with her. She silenced the buzzing phone and flipped it over, her mother's voice already too loud in her head.

You have to do this for us, darling.

Surely, you wouldn't abandon us in our time of greatest need, would you? Could you?

She shuddered. How was it always *her* job to fix the problems her parents got themselves into?

Because Nora's death left that responsibility to you, her overeager subconscious chimed in. Another tremor coursed through her as she considered this loss on top of all the others.

She waved the bartender over. "I changed my mind. I'll have another."

She stole a glance at her Hermes watch even though she knew the exact amount of time she had left. Only four days of freedom. Not nearly enough. Urgency tickled her throat. She attempted to squelch it with a healthy gulp of her refreshed martini, but it barely made a dent.

She'd be home in less than a week. They could talk then.

The handsome stranger moved toward her, his predatory gaze pinned to hers. He still spoke to whoever was on the phone, but they held a fraction of his interest. His focus was *her. And so the hunted became the hunter.* Fine. She could give him that. As long as she got to feed.

"Sorry," he mouthed.

She shook her head. "No biggie. I'm not going anywhere," she whispered.

His smile lit up the dark bar and simultaneously sent a chill racing down her skin.

"*Sí, claro. No quiero nada sin…* certain assurances," he said into the phone, extending his hand for her to take.

Well, if that voice wasn't just as sexy as the man using it, she'd fly home right then.

"Hi. I'm—" he started but then growled into the phone. "*No, absolutamente no.*"

He took her hand in his and kissed the top of it. *Good grief. This man is sex in sandals.* Adding to her warmth, a small flicker of desire ignited when she caught his gaze, a piercing stare searing her with liquid-blue heat. Those crystal-azure eyes… the way they glowed as if made of the stars and sea. He kept her hand in his, rubbing circles on the pad of her palm while he nodded into the phone like the person on the other end could see him.

Hmmmm. He is adorable. Another rub she could feel in her bones. *And interested.*

"Don't go anywhere," he whispered, covering the receiver with his hand. "Sorry. Family." He pointed to the phone, and she held her own up, boasting twenty-three missed texts and two missed calls on her home screen.

"That's why I don't answer," she whispered back conspiratorially.

"*Mierda.* No… No! *Escúchame, Papá…*" He paused, pinching the bridge of his nose while she took in his features up close. Good Lord, he was handsome.

The flame in her stomach moved south, growing into a blazing inferno as he appraised her, raking his gaze over her exposed skin. He winked before licking full, crimson lips set against tanned brown skin. If only she knew the Spanish word for hot as sin.

She followed his lips down along a square jaw, tracing his profile with her eyes. His pronounced chin gave way to a muscled neck, then cut shoulders, and finally sinewy biceps that looked capable of lifting a house.

Oh, yeah. You may not know it yet, but you're about to be mine.

She gulped back a wave of lust as his arms wrapped around her semi-bare waist.

Why him? Her subconscious asked.

Why not?

His sculpted arms were all the more pronounced by the tank top he wore advertising a local beer. *Interesting.* The shirt was at odds with the power he exuded, though. Because there was no way he was local. Or a beach guy, either. T-shirt be damned.

When he hung up the phone and focused all his attention on her, a shiver ran over her exposed skin. Boy, had she underestimated his intensity.

His scent mixed with the thick ocean air, wrapping her in a musk that was one hundred percent masculine. A hint of spice—Cypress and Pine—snaked up her nostrils, invading her senses. For a moment, she forgot who she was and why she was there. Her knees gave out, but his arms steadied her, drew her closer.

"Sorry about that. My family is a little… intense." Yep. That accent was a hundred percent Spanish. *Dios, indeed.*

"No problem. We've got time. Besides, if anyone understands intense family, it's me."

"Well, then maybe we should run away together and never come back," he teased. He paused and gestured for her to introduce herself.

"Lissa. And I'll come any time you want," she replied haughtily, gesturing with a mimicked wave of her hand that she'd like his name as well. Tit for tat, or something to that effect. She rarely gave anything without expecting at least equal in return. Part of her genetic makeup.

"I'm Gael. And I'll keep that in mind. Do you have a last name, Lissa?"

"Not one I care to share."

He laughed then, a full, throaty guffaw that filled the open-air space.

"Well, Lissa with no last name, may I buy you a drink?" he asked, setting his empty bottle on the bar top in front of her.

"Why not? A vodka martini. Dirty. Extra dirty," she added, tossing him a wink.

"But, of course. To our health," he said when their drinks were set in front of them. His breath was close enough to her skin to warm it, and his thick, Spanish accent rolled over her like a full-bodied Chianti. Damn, he was sexy. He knew it too. The glint in his eyes suggested he thought he was in control of the situation.

Silly man. He'd find out soon enough how wrong he was.

"To tonight," she countered.

He nodded, not taking his gaze off her as they both sipped at their drinks. The temperature was dropping by the minute, which meant the rain would come earlier than the weatherman had asserted. Not that it mattered in the least. A full-blown hurricane could come crashing in and she wouldn't care as long as he didn't stop staring at her like that.

"And after?"

"I've got a… family engagement that will keep me out of the game."

"Well, it's a good thing I've got my own… family issues to attend to. What's the engagement?"

She smiled up at him and ran her finger along his stubbled jawline, wishing it were her lips tracing him.

"Since you ask," she said, tucking a lock of his curly, espresso-colored locks behind his ear. All it would take was a step up on her toes to claim his mouth, to taste him once and for all. Her skin buzzed with electricity. "I'm a princess, and, well, you know the drill. Blah, blah, blah. It's all so drab."

His jaw tightened, his eyes raging with a storm of his own. "Let me guess, you have to marry a prince?"

She forced a laugh and shrugged. "A king, actually.

First-world problems, huh?" The facts were less believable than anything she could pull from her imagination, but saying it out loud still stung. She sealed the truth-posed-as-lie with a wink and leaned in, brushing her lips against his as lightly as she could.

He laughed again, this time an altogether huskier sound that settled low in her stomach, making it flip.

"What a shame I didn't meet you sooner. See, I'm a prince on his way to being king, and could have swept you off your feet. Screw that other guy."

"Sounds like treason, mister." She trailed a finger along his angular jaw, tempted to keep going along his collarbone and south. "And yes, a damned shame indeed. Stupid ol' fate is always getting it wrong, isn't she? Anyway, if you're up for some fun, I'm here until Friday." Her finger made its way to his chest, solid and warm. "Take it or leave it."

He seemed to consider her proposal, pausing before he answered, but not long enough for her to doubt his interest. "I'll take it. All of it." A challenge was issued in his eyes, in his arms that wrapped around her waist, closing the last of the distance between them.

She closed her eyes and cinched her hands around his neck, pulling him into her.

"Good choice."

She brought her lips to his and ran her tongue along his bottom lip, knowing that exquisite pleasure for herself at last. He tasted of orange blossom and vanilla, and damn if she didn't almost come right there.

As the rain began to fall, Lissa tangled her fingers in his hair. She had three days of freedom in front of her, and she intended to use each and every one to ravish the beautiful man whose taste was still on her tongue.

She might have to kiss a frog in less than a week, but she was going to bed with Mr. Charming tonight.

CHAPTER ONE: PRESENT DAY

Gael's face raged with heat, and his fists were pinned tight against his side in an effort to temper his anger. His father's study, lined with Spanish teak wood and enough gold to summon Midas, was not the place to be having this conversation. Hell, he didn't want to have it at all.

"I am not repeating this argument, Papá. We've been through it more than once."

"*Sí*, but—" his father started.

"No. But nothing. I made my choice. Two years ago. Not a damn thing has changed. Tomás agreed to step up as Prince. I'm more than pleased with my role in the military."

Gael picked up a gold-plated pen that probably cost more than their chef made in a month. The temptation to throw the thing across the room was almost strong enough to follow through.

"But for *what*? You're chasing a ghost, *hijo*. You don't even know her last name. Don't you understand how… how ludicrous this all is? To give it all up for love?"

It might look ludicrous to someone else, but *Dio*. He

didn't *just* want love, either. Not anymore. He wanted *her*.

Lissa.

She'd claimed him with her body, first—and what a body it was. Tall, curvaceous as if she was born of the *peligroso* S-curves of the Andes. Strong as the sun glinting off the Mediterranean, but soft in all the right places. And her hair. Oh, her hair and her skin, one made of fire, the other ice.

But none of that compared to her mind, her wit, her innate knowledge of what made him tick. Every touch, every whisper, every rock of her hips called to him still, like a siren pulling him into the deep.

"So, we're really doing this, Papá? Fine. What do you possibly think you can say that will change my mind?"

His father, the king, spit with rage at his eldest son, listing all the reasons his decision to give up the throne was short-sighted and foolish.

Money. Duty. Responsibility.

Every argument his father made, Gael countered.

He didn't need the money.

He didn't give a damn about duty.

The kingdom—and arranged marriage that went with it—wasn't his responsibility and hadn't been for some time.

"So, what is this about, then?" his father asked. "What could you possibly have to offer her?"

"I love her, and I'll make a life for us either way. And I *will* find her, Papá." Not that his father gave a damn if love was involved or not. While Gael might not do casual relationships, his father had preached about nothing else since Gael was old enough to hear it. They were the only way for a royal to get certain… needs met.

Gael had other ideas, one to satisfy those needs and an ache for something more at the same time.

"You haven't even found her yet."

As if that could stop him. "*Yet.* But who says I'm done looking?"

"And if she disappeared on purpose? What if she doesn't want anything more from you? You have to consider that possibility, son. Before it's too late."

Gael shook his head. *No. That isn't possible.* Not after what they'd shared… But the thought lingered, malignant and necrotic, wearing his resolve.

The truth was, it didn't matter. He'd been marked a changed man after she'd walked out of his suite on day four of their screwfest, her *toro*-red curls and Mediterranean-green eyes both wild. She hadn't even said goodbye, just pried his mouth open with her tongue, kissed him within an inch of his life, and walked out the door. She'd tossed back four words that he still called back in the loneliness of the cold, dark nights of the Galician winter.

It's been fun, amor.

Fun. Ha! As if that could begin to describe the four-day affair. He'd come home and abdicated his throne, passing off responsibility to his younger brother. Not just the kingdom, either. He gave up everything that went with it.

The money, the title, his future.

Because what kind of a future could it be without her?

And that—the utter loss of his sanity after only four days with the woman—was precisely why he didn't do hookups. Not that it mattered. He'd broken his singular rule and was paying for it now.

"You'll lose your title," his father tried again.

Gael pinched the bridge of his nose, frustration settling in his chest like sand, heavy and grating. "I already did. I haven't been involved in anything related to the crown in two years, Papá. In fact, I've been meaning to talk to you about that. I want a permanent position in the royal military. There's precedent with Sir Michél. 1948."

His father ignored him and went on with his tirade. "What about your finances? You'll no longer have access to the royal funds you're accustomed to."

"Papá, you and I both know with my own accounts, I'll

never have to work again if I don't want to. Neither will my children, or their children. I'll be fine."

"You won't be King."

"*Jesús.* Haven't you been listening? I never wanted it to begin with. Not a day in my life. Tomás has, though, and he's been preparing the past two years. Think about it. Do you want to hand over your country to a man who will only take the position out of duty, or would you rather make sure it's in the hands of someone with a passion for the role, the land, the title?"

That silenced his father, but the tall, stately man hadn't budged. He just stood there, stoically appraising his eldest son who refused to waive under the intense stare. Gael knew what he wanted and wouldn't stop until he got it.

"Son," he tried again, but Gael waved him off.

"No. Enough. Tell me this, Papá—has an arranged marriage made you happy or at least made you a better king? Because if it has done either of those, fine. I'll bite the bullet and walk down whatever aisle you need me to. But I think, if you could do it over, you'd have done it differently."

Finally, futility settled over the King. Everyone knew he took up with as many affairs as he could afford without being blatantly obvious about his indiscretions, while Gael's mother pretended not to notice by diving head first into renovating the décor of the palace every six months.

The King nodded at first, in subtle but tacit agreement, only to break off into the only spontaneous fit of laughter Gael had ever seen him make. He shook with joy or madness, Gael couldn't be sure which, finally clapping his son on the shoulder.

"You're right about that, son. More than you know. I'll alert Tomás about the sword he'll be expected to fall upon on your behalf. *¿Bien?*"

Gael opened his mouth to thank his father for— *finally!*—hearing him, when the door to the study opened. Tomás, his younger brother by ten years, strode through, a tumbler of amber liquid in his hands.

"Speak of the Devil." Gael smiled and met his brother halfway through the entrance, embracing him with a firm hug. "Good to see you again, *hermanito*. You look good. Almost old enough to wear that shit on your lapel." He flicked the royal medals that explained what his brother had been up to since he last came home. Apparently, a lot.

"Well, well, well. Look what the monsoons brought in. I didn't think you were coming to this circus," Tomás quipped. He squeezed Gael tighter. "But I'm glad you did. Someone needs to drink me through this thing."

"Stay out of my wine, son," the King ordered, but Tomás ignored him. "You need to be sober when you meet your future in-laws."

"Yeah, yeah. Anyway, what brought you here, *hermano*? I really did think you were training."

Gael shrugged. "This guy said he had some things to talk to me about, and you know I can't refuse a meeting with the King." He winked, and the two brothers shared a laugh.

"I'm going downstairs. I hate it when you two talk about me as if I'm not here. Be good and don't be late, Tomás."

Tomas smiled, and when he was out of direct sight of their dad, winked at his brother.

"You hear something, Gael?"

"Nope. You?"

The door to the study slammed shut on Gael and Tomás erupting in a fit of laughter.

"I love messing with the old man. He makes it too easy."

"That's the truth. So, tell me, *hermano*, why're you really here? We weren't expecting you. Not that I'm not happy to have you around or anything. I meant what I said about you needing to help me drink my way through this."

Tomás made his way to a tall cabinet and unlocked it with a key he procured from a hidden breast pocket.

"Shhh. I made a copy last year when Papá got drunk at a state dinner and asked me to bring him a bottle of 'Spain's finest.'"

Gael nodded his approval.

"Genius. Wish I'd thought of it when I lived here. Anyway, I was honest before. Papá wanted to talk, so I flew up."

Gael had been stationed down south at the Grenada Naval Base for the past eighteen months and only came home when summoned. Sometimes not even then. He missed his brother, but dealing with his father's relentless queries about his choices wasn't worth the trip most times.

"He try and talk you out of giving it all up again?"

"Yeah, but I think this time I got him to see things my way."

Tomás grinned, a wicked glint in his eyes as he procured a bottle of rioja from the felt-lined cabinet and opened it. After a final gulp of whatever he'd had in the glass before, he filled it with ruby-red wine—yes, one of Spain's finest—and handed it over to his brother before taking a swig out of the bottle.

"How'd you manage that? I feel like I should be taking notes."

"I just reminded him that an arranged marriage never did anyone in this family any favors. Love couldn't make things any worse, could it?"

Tomás laughed and took another long pull from the bottle of wine. God, Gael missed the kid. Maybe he could be around more now that things were settled with his father and Tomás could finally take the role he'd been vying for since he was a child.

"Dang. I mean, I'm impressed but surprised he gave in. Remember Papá's face when you told him you were trading it all in for her the first time?" Tomás barked out a laugh.

"I thought his head was going to explode. I wish someone would've filmed that. What was it he said? That she wasn't worth it? I almost threw our whole relationship in the trash right there."

That was an understatement. He'd been close to clocking his father—too close.

"I think he said, 'This is why you're giving up the life I made for you? A woman? A woman you can't even locate? It's been months, *years* since the affair.' I mean, he wasn't wrong."

"No, but it wasn't his decision to make. Still isn't."

"Glad you two are still talking, though. That you're okay otherwise. I mean, you are, aren't you?"

Gael nodded. "More than okay, thanks. I love my life, Tomás, I really do."

He'd left the palace that day two years ago and never looked back. He'd never been drawn to the throne like his younger brother, longing instead for a life outside the palace walls, where travel and adventure ruled his days. Commanding a fleet in the Navy gave him an ample dose of both, adding on the ability to make hands-on change for his country, a far more enticing prospect than the politics of ruling it.

And yet…

An ache welled up inside him, gaping and festering more every day since the day he'd flown home from the Kelles. The only thing that would fill it and heal what hurt was Lissa. He'd never been more sure of anything.

He'd even recently finished a project in the Pyrenees with her in mind. Not even Tomás was aware of it.

"Not to take sides with Papá, but are you absolutely sure this is what you want? Because after today, you don't have a choice. Hell, neither of us do."

Gael sighed and took a sip of the wine, then let it roll around his mouth, appreciating the tartness. He absently ran his hand along his father's desk as he let the wine slide down his throat. It wasn't the same teak wood as the bar where he'd met Lissa, but it might as well have been the way the memories of that night pulled at his thoughts, distracting him from whatever his brother was saying. He shut his eyes against them, hoping they'd dissipate, but they only grew in intensity.

He saw flashes of red and green, then alabaster skin bared for his eager hands behind his closed lids. Now that the memories surfaced, he wasn't sure he wanted them to go since they were his only link to her, and a poor substitute at that.

"Hey, Gael. You in there somewhere?" Tomás asked.

Gael nodded but pressed his eyes together tighter, hoping to hang on to the images, but like always, they evaporated and disappeared like his breath on the frigid Pyrenees winds.

"Yeah. Just thinking about your question."

"Bull. You were thinking about her, weren't you?"

"Same thing. Tomás, I can't even consider taking a job or a life that would mean I have to give up looking for her. It's impossible to explain, but she's it. I can just feel it."

"You need to get laid, buddy, and fast. This kind of obsession isn't healthy."

He'd tried that, though, and it was as futile as the rest of it. He had all the right tools—the royal name, a near-royal fortune, some decent looks if he could humbly say so, not to mention the uniform marking him amongst the elite in the Spanish Navy—but it didn't matter. None of the women had what he needed.

Some drew him in with a shade of red hair close to Lissa's, but it always appeared drab compared to the shimmering flames Lissa wore like a crown of fire.

Others caught his gaze with green eyes, but upon closer inspection, they were just that, *green*. Not jade jewels set in the most perfect creamy skin a man could imagine, skin that trailed all the way down her chest, her taut stomach… *Ugh*. The bottom line?

They weren't *her*. So, they'd never measure up.

"Not gonna happen, but thanks for the helpful suggestion."

"Fine, but one more thing, Gael. You slept with the woman for half a week and she never told you her last name. You don't find that odd?"

"Not you, too."

Tomás threw his hands up in defeat. "I just want you to think through all the angles. You're giving up a lot for a woman who doesn't seem to want to be found is all I'm saying."

"I'm giving up more if I stop looking. I want love, a life shared between partners, not a smashing together of names and titles to force prosperity on kingdoms who've done fine before I got here."

Gael smiled, but his chest hurt with all the talk about the past two years and how fruitless his search had been. Lissa had done more than just upend his vacation two years ago. Meeting her, *loving* her, had permanently and bindingly altered the course of his life. If he was ever uncertain about whether or not he could marry for convenience—not his, but his country's, his parents'—meeting her had solidified his decision.

"Yeah, well, you always were the romantic, big brother. As for me, I'm gonna head downstairs when I'm done with this wine and meet the woman whose name I'm going to smash together with mine to force prosperity on our kingdoms."

"Hey, I didn't mean—" Gael began, but his brother cut him off with a shake of his head.

"No. Don't. I know what you mean, but I knew what taking the crown entailed. I'm assuming the role of King, and I don't take that lightly."

"Still, I'm sorry. God, Tom, I'm such an *imbécile*. I came home from that trip and acted on every damned emotion, every desire. And then I left without even checking that you were okay. Jesus. I didn't even consider how much I'd wreck your plans, your..."

Tomás silenced him with a gentle hand on his shoulder.

"Stop with the martyr crap," Tomás said, his old smile

laced with mischief replacing the serious one from moments ago. "I just wanted to give you a hard time. You haven't wrecked anything other than my piss-poor image, and if I'm being honest, I'm grateful for it. I was having fun, sure, but it wasn't fulfilling. More than anything, it was a way to pass the time 'til I found my calling. You just sped up the process a bit."

"You're not pissed? I was pretty selfish."

"Nah. You had the right to be. I might have been a little annoyed when Papá came to tell me just before Natasha showed up, but again, if I'm sticking with the truth? I was always jealous of you. I wanted the gig, so when I heard you didn't, I was jazzed. You made my year, big brother. But if you don't mind me asking, why'd you wait 'til now to have this little chat?"

Why had he? Because he'd been scared of the answer. Because he wasn't going to change his mind, no matter how his brother felt about it. Still, it had been the coward's way out.

"I don't know. But I won't make that mistake again. You've changed, *hermanito*. In a good way."

"Shhh. You make me sound like I'm turning into Papá. I'm still a little fun." As if to prove it, he downed the rest of the wine and pulled the bottle away, grinning. "Anyway, Papá's gonna read us the riot act if we're late. So, here, grab one of these boxes."

Gael took the box of what looked like champagne flutes from Tomás.

"What're these for?"

"The party. Duh. Why did you think Papá called you back now? He wanted to be sure you knew what you were doing before the festivities kicked off."

"Party? What party?" His brother's birthday wasn't for another two months.

"Uh, my Adios-to-the-single-ladies party. Don't pretend you didn't remember to get out of sending me a gift. And I expect nothing short of a killer stag party, too.

Start planning, *hermano*."

"*Mierda*. That's still happening?"

The party his brother referred to was his engagement party. The sham marriage was now squarely sitting on his shoulders, and all Gael could do was watch from the sidelines.

"Of course. Party tomorrow, wedding in a month. You really didn't know?"

"Nope. I thought you were kidding when you said you were going downstairs to meet your wife. I didn't think that was still going to happen when I gave up the crown. But if you think I'm leaving, you've got another thing coming. You've had my back, and now it's my turn to have yours. Now spill. How's this all happening?"

"Okay, I'm stealing another bottle of wine if we're opening this can of worms. Plus, I'm hoping to be a little buzzed when we're introduced tonight. You know, wine goggles and all that. I heard she's like ten years older than me. Gross." He laughed, but Gael's heart felt like it had been snapped with a whip.

Tonight? His brother was meeting the woman he was supposed to love, cherish, and honor for eternity tonight, only to marry her in a month? *Dio*. And she was Gael's age? Failure rippled through his body like a quake he couldn't control.

Tomás led the way to his suite, where he demanded of his valet that a bottle of wine—damned good wine from his father's actually hidden stash, he'd specified as if the palace was in the habit of serving drivel—be brought immediately.

"*Vale*, so what's with this sudden interest in my well-being? You've been gone most of the past two years. You're acting odd, Gael. Well, odder than usual." Tomás grinned with mischief.

"I just can't believe they're holding you to that ancient concept. I thought after my tirade they'd have at least given it some thought. As if any of them found happiness that way. And isn't that why treaties and alliances are built? So royalty is kept out of it?"

"You'd think, but I don't mind. It's part of the gig, and besides, married men—nay, *kings*—are the ultimate aphrodisiac to young, helpless women. Look at Papá." His brother passed the flippant comment off as a joke, but Gael didn't find any part of this humorous. Their father's galivanting and cavorting was part of why Gael didn't have any desire for hookups, a rule he'd followed until he laid eyes on Lissa.

"You're going to cheat around on your wife? Papá isn't exactly a role model in that regard."

"It's not cheating if you make an agreement, Gael. Don't be as old-fashioned as Mamá. I'm betting my future bride will want the same agreement. No way she's a thirty-year-old virgin. She'll have desires of her own a twenty-year-old won't be able to fulfill. Am I right? Besides, I'm not worried about it, so you shouldn't be."

How was there so much Gael hadn't considered when it came to his brother's role as future King? As a husband?

But he was in it now, like it or not.

"Jesus, Tomás, how are you going to marry someone you don't love?"

"I knew what I was signing on to when you abdicated. Now, can you please stop worrying? We only have an hour 'til we meet her and I want to be good and drunk by then."

Gael laughed, but stones of doubt fell to his stomach, settling there and weighing down his thoughts. He sipped on his wine while his brother got dressed and downed three-quarters of the second bottle of Rioja himself.

Tomás wondered aloud what his bride—some royal cousin to the Aldonian King, a princess herself—would look like. His only request was that she wasn't a "total hound" so he could enjoy making heirs with her. And *there* was the younger brother Gael recalled from their youth. He chuckled at his brother's physically-driven priorities, always more in line with his father's than Gael's. Tomás always was a playboy, and honestly, it was good to see him lighthearted on what would be one of the more inauspicious days of his life.

The heavy wooden door to the suite slammed open just as Tomás was about to order a third bottle of rioja, crashing into the stone wall behind it.

"*Jesús Cristo, Papá.* You're still in charge, so you're paying for it if you break my door down."

His father didn't crack a smile, but Gael bit one back. Good for Tomás. He needed to take the piss wherever he could before he was tied to the crown, the bride, and the job.

"You're drunk." At least his father knew well enough not to pose that as a question.

"I am, but don't worry, I won't embarrass anyone."

"Nothing we can do about it now. Let's go, we're running late. Not the impression we hope to make. Are you coming along as well, Gael?"

Gael nodded. He wasn't going to miss the show now that he had a front-row seat to the three-ring circus it'd become. At least it would be a good story to tell the men back at the barracks as they toasted their own freedom to marry whomever the hell they chose.

"C'mon, Papá," Tomás said, swallowing back a hiccup. "I'm giving her the rest of my life. Surely, she can give me five minutes to straighten my tie?"

The King stormed out, muttering under his breath something about his *hijos tontos,* leaving the brothers alone.

Gael was about to launch into a speech about how his brother could call him any time he needed, that he would be there for him in all the ways he hadn't been when they'd been younger, but Tomás shook his head.

"I'll be fine. No grand speeches now. You'll ruin my buzz." Tomás's smile wavered for half a second but was back in place before Gael could comment on it.

"Let's go, then," Gael ordered, corralling his brother toward the exit. "I can't wait to meet the lucky lady who gets to put up with your crap the rest of her life."

Ten minutes later, they were all lined up in the throne room, the air heavy with anticipation. It was ornately, if not ostentatiously, decorated with the flags of their nation, their clans and their history, not to mention every suit of armor their military had ever worn on full display. It was a show of money, of power, and was chosen purposefully for this occasion, rather than the more modest, delicate sitting room.

What a joke. It was yet another moment to throw into stark contrast the difference between the life Gael was born into and the one he wanted for himself.

Circus, indeed.

When his gaze focused on the family opening the doors and walking toward him, though, everything changed in one rapid beat of his heart. His world shifted off its axis and tumbled away from him faster than he could catch it. His head spun, and dizziness consumed him. His mouth went dry, and his palms trembled like the Pyrenean oaks in autumn.

No. *No, no, no.*

He noticed the hair first, like a cascade of fire coming to devour him where he stood. He'd happily have died under those flames. Then the eyes, the jade-green orbs that took in the ornate marble and carved stone throne room with unhidden surprise. His gaze trailed over the rest of her as it had the day he'd first laid eyes on her. The body he was intimately aware of—every curve and peak and valley—was just as stunning in a floor-length emerald silk dress as it had been sheathed in what could barely be considered a dress in the islands. If anything, she filled out the formal shift far better than the casual beach clothes he'd seen her in previously. When she'd had clothes on at all, that was.

But his brain refused to believe what his eyes were one-hundred percent certain of.

It was Lissa, in the flesh.

It *couldn't* be her, could it? Life surely wasn't that wicked, the world that small. Because it looked like he'd scoured the planet for years only to have her arrive at his doorstep, as if that had always been the plan.

Let's screw each other senseless and then meet up in a couple of years at your palace. Sound good?

Had he missed a step somewhere?

There was no doubt, not in his heart that recognized her immediately. It pounded furiously, desperate to race to her, but his feet remained cemented in place.

Dios mio. She was there. Not a mirage, not a figment of his hyperactive imagination where she was concerned. But *there*, in his palace. His brother's palace, technically, but his family's all the same.

But how? *Why?* All the searching, all the missed opportunities to locate her, all of it came crashing down around him with the crushing realization that she was standing right in front of him.

Finally. Less than a meter away. Hell, who cared why?

He watched the other men in the room pale with lust as they took in the sight of her. Even his brother's jaw was unhinged, tongue practically lolling out of his mouth.

Jealousy pushed out the joy at having rediscovered her and roiled loud and angrily in his chest, clawing to get out.

She wasn't theirs to ogle. She was *his*.

He attempted a move in her direction—he had to let her know he was there—but she kept moving, gliding like a bodiless spirit across the marble floor away from him and toward his father. She tossed Gael a glance, one laced with surprise, followed by a visual dressing down. Her lips were pursed, her snowy skin flushed a pale pink.

She was gorgeous, animated, but pissed, too. At him, if he read her look correctly. His pulse sped up, registering a warning. But of what?

She shook her head and broke his gaze without more than a passing glance.

What the—?

The dismissal stung, burned in the place along his heart she'd branded him. She was his, dammit. She'd claimed him wholly and completely and in taming his wild sexual appetites, traded ownership of his heart. What the actual hell was she playing at by pretending none of that had happened?

Before he could make a move toward her, a trumpet blared. Even though he was expecting it on some level, chains secured tightly around his heart when his father rose to meet Lissa, bowing his head to the man on her left, most likely her father. He only did that with royalty.

Which meant...

"Princess Elisabeth, King Edward, Queen Joya. What a pleasure to meet you all. Please allow me the pleasure of introducing you to my family. This is Gael, Capitán of our Highness's Royal Navy."

Gael froze as her gaze met his, this time, lingering a second longer than was tradition before she dipped her head and bowed. An electric charge powerful enough to light the kingdom for a month passed between them before she froze over, a thin smile on her face.

"Elisabeth, is it?" Was that why she'd chosen the nickname when they met? A cloak of anonymity?

"Elisabeth, yes. It's a pleasure, Señor." Her jaw was tight, a smile fastened in place. But the way her eyebrows were raised in recognition meant she knew damn well who he was and refused to show it.

Wait. That's it? That's all I get?

His heart cracked down the middle as she moved on to his brother, a bright smile illuminating her face, a thin red veil of color burnishing her cheeks.

"And this is your future husband, my son, Prince Tomás of España."

She bowed again, deep and courteous, her cascading curls tumbling like a fiery waterfall around her face and shielding her from Gael's vision.

And that was when he understood everything as clearly

as the storm-sheltered lagoon he and Lissa had made love in on their last night.

She was to be his brother's bride. A princess for the prince. A queen for the future king.

No. No, no, no, no, no! The echoes of his dissent rattled off the walls of his skull, giving him an instant headache.

As much as he hoped, prayed, and begged for it not to be true, he knew it was.

She'd been telling the truth the night they met—she was a princess engaged to marry a king. But of course she was. Of course, fate would be this merciless and cold-hearted, because if he hadn't met her, he would've remained in line for the throne, and it would be *him* accepting and kissing the top of her hand as his brother did now, *him* marrying her in less than a month's time.

Him spending the rest of his life loving the woman who'd stolen his heart two years ago.

Damn fate, the vicious and heartless mistress.

He couldn't stay there in that room she sucked the very life out of, not without saying or doing something unforgivable. He stormed toward the exit of the throne room, fury, jealousy, and a pain so severe it almost dropped him to his knees blinding him from the stares of his family and court.

He didn't care what they thought of him. Nothing mattered anymore.

Only one thought was able to push through the tangled mess of emotions spiraling out of control in his head.

He'd made a royal mistake two years ago, one he'd pay for the rest of his life.

CHAPTER TWO

Lissa's heart thumped so loudly in her chest that she worried the whole line of strangers in front of her would hear it echo against the towering granite and marble walls in the capacious room. She felt her father's eyes burning a hole in her cheek, but she didn't dare break eye contact with the Spanish King to meet his gaze. It would be filled with either questions or disappointment, and she didn't have the time or mental space for either.

Not while every cell, every one of her senses was focused on one thing, and one thing only.

Gael.

"What was that about?" her mother hissed.

Oh, nothing, Lissa wanted to say, *just the man I slept with when I ran away two years ago.*

A line of sweat beaded on her brow and she thanked whatever gods there were that she'd chosen a dress that would hide all manner of sin, the dampness that grew on her stomach, her chest, along her hips included.

The man she'd attempted to use to assuage the pain of a life stunted by her ladder-climbing parents was there, in the same room as her, or had been until he'd fled as fast as if the room had been engulfed in flames. In a way, it was.

Or at least it felt like it.

"This is ridiculous. Offensive, really," her mother continued.

Lissa let out a small hiss of annoyance. Her mother wouldn't know offensive if it bit her on the backside. "Where is he? The brother?"

Where is he, indeed?

His absence took all the air from the room just as his presence had moments ago. Her brain still hadn't caught up to her heart and figured out what twist of fate had gone so terribly wrong that she'd found him again, only to be pawned off on his brother, a future King. A younger brother, too, from the looks of it.

No, none of this could be possible.

And yet… there they were. His scent—the Cypress and Pine she'd let infect her like a disease when they were shacked up the last four days of her trip to the Kelles Islands—lingered behind, all but suffocating her with desire.

"This is uncalled for. Somebody better bring that boy back," her father threatened.

Lissa bit her lip to keep from volunteering for the task.

Suddenly, without warning, the memories she'd tried like hell to push back to the recesses of her mind came sprinting to the forefront of her thoughts.

Catching his gaze from across the bar the first night they made love.

His mess of curls, dark and coarse and seated at the center of her desire.

His eyes, filled with hurt when she'd left him with nothing more than a kiss and a few parting words.

What he hadn't seen, the part of this memory that crushed into her chest with brute force, was the way she'd fallen to her knees and sobbed when she got back to her room to pack for her departure.

And now?

She shivered as a pool of moisture slipped from the

part of her that remembered how good his tongue, his fingers, and his length had felt that night and the other two as well. They'd melded so well together. Nothing she'd found before or since could measure up.

Dammit.

It wasn't supposed to be more than a fun couple of nights of good sex, a stolen moment in exchange for all the moments that would be robbed from her in the future. She didn't do serious relationships, not with all their messy trappings of love and emotions she couldn't reciprocate.

But, despite her best intentions, she'd fallen head over heels for the man.

"Elisabeth," her father jeered.

She startled. All eyes were on her as if awaiting a response to a question she hadn't heard.

The future King, her future husband, had a look of amusement on his face, his smile crooked but kind, if not laced with mischief. He was handsome, sure, sharing many of the same qualities as his older sibling, but something was missing—the decade that would bridge their ages notwithstanding.

You love someone else. Of course he isn't enough.

That was true, but so was the fact that he, not his brother, was meant to be her groom. The sooner she realized that and moved on from Gael, the better. Her heart knocked against her ribcage, screeching at her for ignoring what was painfully obvious.

She'd never be over Gael.

But she could forget him, at least enough to make a decent life with his brother. Hadn't she been practicing that her entire life? Pushed everyone away because her future wasn't hers to give?

"Excuse me. I felt dizzy for a moment. Would you mind repeating the question?"

Her father barked out a cough laced with animosity. A chill crept up her spine despite the warmth radiating from the blazing fire in the hearth and the stone walls.

"Our hosts have expressed how nice it is to have you here," he muttered through gritted teeth. "I suggest you reply now, *dear*, or face my wrath if your brainlessness messes this up for us."

Lissa flinched, causing her to bite her tongue and taste the metallic reminder of her father's cruelty. At least when she was married off, she wouldn't be under his scrutiny anymore.

"It's a pleasure meeting you as well. And my deepest apologies, but will you please direct me to your powder room? I'm still feeling faint and would like to splash some water on my face before we sit for dinner."

She ignored her father's protestations and smiled when Tomás offered to show her the way. He led her from the room silently, but she could feel his relentless gaze just as she had her father's earlier. Tomás's was much gentler, at least.

"What is it, Your Majesty?" she finally asked outside the doors, turning to look at him. *Different. He's different from Gael.*

He shared his brother's square jaw, but his nose and eyes were softer, less pronounced. He was shorter than Gael, barely an inch taller than her in her heels. His smile didn't light up, didn't let her into his soul the way Gael's had, either.

But she was right in her initial assessment of him. He was handsome as sin and probably did quite well with the ladies before his freedom had been stripped from him as it had her. And at such a young age. That one small detail gave her solace. At least she wasn't alone in this.

"You seem familiar. Have we met?"

She chuckled. "No, but I'm surprised you think a pick-up line is necessary, my liege. You know this is a sure thing, don't you? Our parents have seen to that."

He laughed, a loud guffaw that echoed down the narrow hallway they found themselves in.

"You're a pistol. This should be fun. Though, I wasn't

trying for suave. You really do seem as if I know you. But I'd have recalled your hair, your eyes…" He trailed off, appraising her with an eager gaze.

Her skin erupted in goose pimples as she ignored the veiled compliment. The air was cooler out here, but it was trepidation about how much to share with him—he was to be her husband after all—that sent her body into a trembling tailspin. If she told Tomás about her affair with Gael, or confirmed it, it could ruin the engagement.

"Thank you, Your Grace. At least, I think. I appreciate you accompanying me out here, but I assure you I'm fine now. You can return and I'll just be a moment behind you."

As soon as I figure out where your brother is. He has some explaining to do.

But after that? She had to let him go.

"Not on my watch, Princess. I'd hate it if I left you out here all alone and something happened to you. They can wait until we get back. Take your time. I'm not going anywhere."

No, he wasn't, was he? She sighed.

"Thank you, again, Your Grace. Your kindness knows no bounds."

This was it, then. The death of her freedom. The end of any hope of getting out of this so she could be with Gael. She feared going home to her parents' estate empty-handed more than those losses, though. At least she'd have Gael in her life in some capacity if she married his brother.

That had to count for something.

Yeah, right. You love him. Something *will never be good enough.*

Too bad. It would have to be.

Before she could think of a lie—anything to steal a moment alone to search for Gael—he strode down the cavernous corridor toward them, his jaw set and eyes no more than feral slits. His year-round tan still draped his forehead and neck, but his cheeks had turned a deep purple as if they'd been burned.

"Well, well, aren't you two getting on just great. How splendid for the new king and his *bride*." He all but spat the last word like a curse.

Lissa's nerve endings all fired at once, electric and hot. She knew Gael's voice as well as her own and heard it calling to her in its deep, even cadence almost every night she closed her eyes.

This wasn't it. This was fury given a voice, and for the second time since meeting Gael, a sense of foreboding, of danger, tickled her senses.

"We are, thank you." She upped the ante, leaning her head on Tomás's shoulder, hoping to make a point to Gael. Now was neither the time nor place to discuss their history. She might have been his at one point, but that moment had passed them by.

"Hey, why'd you rush out of there so fast? There a fire I didn't know about?" Tomás asked his brother.

"It was getting a little crowded. I figured no one there would miss me." Gael met and held her gaze as he said this, the anger adding a tremor to his voice.

Lissa broke the invisible, electric link surging between them and gave Gael her lightest, most carefree smile as she linked her elbow in Tomás's.

"I'm just taking a moment to breathe—all this excitement and the thin air up here in the mountains, you know—and then we'll head back in. Would you care to join us?"

It was a challenge—*sit in silence with us, then go back in and pretend everything is okay. Please.*

He didn't smile back, his gaze simmering with heat bubbling just below the surface. The only question was whether or not he would blow up, ruining everything for all three of them. Her pulse raced faster with each second that passed. The air in the room teemed with frenetic energy.

Until, finally, a grin spread across Gael's face. Not a

kind, or even sexy smile like she'd seen before. No, this was a sneer. Her skin prickled with awareness.

"Sure." His gaze pinned hers, the same storm raging in his eyes as the night they'd met. When he released her from his gaze, she exhaled a breath she didn't realize was held captive by his stare. "Tomás, since I leave in the morning, why don't I keep your bride company?" Gael said, his voice suddenly syrupy sweet.

"I'm her fiancé. A little inappropriate for you to remain out here with her, isn't it?"

"Not at all. You go check in with the folks to make sure they're behaving themselves and I'll make sure the Princess is safe. That is my job, after all."

Lissa held her breath while Tomás seemed to consider his brother's request.

Please, she willed him. *I just need half a second to get my bearings with Gael.*

Gael slipped his arm around his brother's shoulder, his skin close enough to Lissa's to warm it. It might be the hardest thing she ever had to do not to lean into him.

"Besides, I'd like to get to know her before I leave. Since I won't be back until the wedding, allow me this moment, would you, brother?"

Tomás shot Gael a glance Lissa couldn't decipher, but he smiled, and some of the worry dissipated from the air around them.

"Sure. I'll see you in a moment, Elisabeth. Don't let this one tell you any stories that may steal you away from me. His heart is taken anyhow. We should all be so lucky as to find what he did on vacation, eh, Gael?"

She nodded, an empty gesture that left space for the pounding in her heart to echo through her chest. What Gael had found on vacation? Surely Tomás didn't mean *her*?

It might be comical if it weren't so damned tragic.

Tomás turned back to the doors and passed through them with no more than a glance in their direction.

Like before, all the oxygen was sucked from the room, leaving Lissa dizzy and disoriented. She never faltered under pressure, but she'd never faced anything like this before, either.

The stillness was heavy, the hallway filled with all the words they both wanted to say. Finally, he broke the silence with a growl that reverberated down the long corridor.

"*Please.* Please tell me you're not here to marry him, Lissa. You can't. Not when I looked for you every day. You can't go through with this."

No introduction, no excitement at seeing her again. Just pain, front and center. But what was it he'd said?

He'd searched for her? Guilt burned the back of her eyelids, forcing liquid heat to fall to her cheeks in the form of tears. That was far more than she'd done. She took the coward's way out, choosing to ignore her feelings that morning.

"We don't have a choice, Gael. This was always going to be the ending for us. I was always arranged to marry someone else. That it's your brother is particularly painful, but it doesn't change the outcome."

"You don't have to. I made my choice, Lissa. You can do the same. Please. Jesus." He strode down the corridor just far enough away from her that she ached for his closeness to return.

Oh, why couldn't it have been him she was engaged to? She would have skipped happily down the aisle toward that future.

Her reply stuck in her throat, too sticky to get out. She swallowed hard, then whispered what she could. "I have to. Whatever choice you made, I don't have it at my disposal. You have no idea what I'm risking even talking to you like this."

He stared at her as if she were a ghost. The whole hall seemed haunted with her mistakes piling up around her.

"I don't understand how we let this happen."

Defeat seemed to settle on Gael's shoulders, and they slumped. God, she wished she could close the inches between them, take his head and press it to her chest to console him in the way he'd consoled her that first night together. He hadn't known what he was doing, but he'd brought her back to life, breathed hope into an otherwise dire, unimaginable scenario.

"Why did it have to be him?" she asked. She wasn't expecting an answer, but she had to ask the question either way.

"It wasn't." Gael's voice had shifted once again, this time weak and barely audible.

"Excuse me?"

She froze when a primal keen tore through Gael's chest, piercing her eardrums and heart with equal power. He slammed his fist against the hard oak door beside him, the only proof he made contact in a resounding crack— not of wood, but of bone—and the resulting howl of pain.

"My God! Gael, are you okay?" she asked. One look at his hand told her what the crack insinuated—it was broken. Likely in more than one place. Whatever inner turmoil he faced, it was enough that a fractured hand didn't do anything to the anguish that remained etched on his face.

"No, but I wasn't before this," he said, gesturing to the injured hand swelling more by the minute. "Jesus, Lissa, what have we done?"

What did he mean, *we*? "You need to get that looked at, Gael. They'll need to set it." She reached out to touch his hand, but he pulled it away from her as if her mere proximity hurt more than the break.

He laughed, a mirthless sound devoid of any humor. "It'll heal, but I won't. I screwed this up, Liss."

"How? You can't help the facts, Gael. We had a good time in the islands, a great time, actually, but it was always going to end this way. Remember? I told you that we couldn't go past those four days. I can't have a

37

relationship, and now you know why. It would always have ended in disappointment. Please stop beating yourself up. Literally."

He shook his head violently, the color returning to his cheeks.

"That's not true. Not remotely. Don't you see? It was *me*, Lissa. *I'm* the older sibling, the one in line to marry and take over the throne. Until I gave it up."

The truth of what he was telling her hit her square against the chest, knocking her back into the stone wall. Without its support, she would have no will to stand on her own, no ability to move whatsoever.

Why? Why did you have to let him in? her subconscious screamed at her, but no louder than her breaking heart as she pieced together the wretched puzzle that was her life.

"Wait. So, you're the reason the ceremony got held up?"

He nodded, confirming suspicions she'd had about why everything had taken longer than expected upon her return.

Then, a horrible thought occurred to her. "But wait, that was after…"

She didn't finish her sentence. She didn't need to, nor could she if she wanted to.

"Yes. It was after I met you. I didn't think for a minute I'd be able to marry another after our…" He paused, and she filled in the brief silence with her agreement, even if it was only in her head. "Our affair. I don't know how you felt about me, but dammit, Lissa, you turned me into a man I could be proud of. I never stopped caring about you, looking for you. And in doing that, I potentially ruined both our lives. Mine for certain. I had everything to give you, but I gave it up. Jesus, this is a clusterf—"

"Why? Why would you do that? I told you I couldn't be with you, that I had to marry a…"

"King. *Me*. Until I gave up the throne for *you*. For love. Don't you see how effed we are?"

She nodded, barely able to swallow, her mouth was so dry. None of this should've happened, he was right, but not about the resulting mess they were in now. She never should have seduced him. Not when she felt the sparks, the electricity before he touched her. She should have known then he was dangerous, that it would change everything to love him.

And it had.

It was supposed to be physical, an affair that sent her off to her arranged marriage with a sense that at least she took advantage of the time she had before her days—and her body—were no longer hers. She'd done exactly what she knew would destroy her armor from the inside—she let him in. In doing so, she set off a chain of events that derailed both their lives.

Because he'd fallen for her, too, and had given up his throne, his family, his inheritance.

And her.

In relinquishing his throne, he'd somehow annoyed fate so much, fate who'd thought she was doing them a solid by throwing them onto the same remote island in the midst of their lowest emotional points, that she'd screwed them over. Big time.

"So, what do we do now? Do we need to tell someone what happened, or…?"

"No. We don't tell anyone. What we did was treason, Lissa. They'll hang us both."

"They couldn't possibly. We didn't know…"

"We did, though. Both of us knew. We didn't know enough not to eff everything up, but we knew enough to make some bad decisions."

"Okay, so like I said. If we don't say anything, how can we make this work between us?"

Because now she was certain they could. They loved each other, and she was supposed to be betrothed to him. Hope fluttered like a juvenile hatchling in her chest.

"Lissa, we don't. That's out of our hands now. You

marry my brother and live happily ever after. That's our only option."

"You've got to be kidding me."

"Oh, I'm serious as a heart attack, *mi querida*."

Something snapped, something that had been wound too tightly all these years.

She'd let fear dictate her life back then, and she had even done it earlier that very day when she didn't break free of her father's grasp and run up to Gael, kissing away the past two years of torment. She'd shoved off men, relationships, even friendships at her parents' request, only to live a half-life filled with more regrets than memories.

Well, no more.

She closed the inches between them, wrapping her arms around his neck and pulling his chest against hers. Lust flushed her system of any other emotion.

He'd grown stronger since she'd last held him. In the islands, he'd been sinewy, muscled, but lean. Now, as his rapid heartbeat thumped against her skin through his military suit, it did so through an added twenty pounds of taut, firm flesh.

A rogue wave of desire rolled over her skin and ignited the flame he'd sparked all those years ago.

"We can't do this," he whispered against her neck, the heat from his breath warming her in spite of the arctic chill of the cold, stone hallway that enveloped them.

She ignored his protestation, stepped up on her toes, and pressed her lips to his cheek that blazed beneath her kiss. He groaned, a guttural sound of pleasure laced with agony that shot straight to her stomach, turning it with need. She slipped lower, brushing her lips over his, relishing in that simple pleasure she'd once taken for granted.

No more of that, either, the taking him for granted. He'd looked for her, given up his life for her and for them. No one had ever fought for her. *Ever*. Even though his search hadn't paid off, he deserved to be rewarded for his efforts.

His groan became a growl as he deepened the kiss, opening her mouth with his tongue and tracing the shape of her lips. A purr erupted from her chest, getting lost in the union of their hunger.

He tasted, smelled, and felt the same, and her body immediately recognized him as the only person to ever satisfy it. She melted into his embrace, wishing time would stop and they could remain there, engulfed in their long-lost passion forever.

When he pulled away, her lips ached almost immediately. They were swollen, and she was certain her normally pale, white skin would show their stolen kiss in red blossoms across her cheeks and chest. She struggled to regain her composure, her breath, neither of which lasted long in Gael's presence.

"We can't do this," he reiterated, this time with power behind his statement. It was the voice she recognized from the islands—strong, confident, regal. How hadn't she recognized who he was when she met him? Maybe not the Prince of Galicia, but a prince nonetheless. Because every cell on his body exuded the raw power some men were just born with.

Men who became kings.

That didn't change the fact that he was using his power to utter the last four words she wanted to hear.

"We can. You already walked away from the job, and believe me, when I get you alone again, I want to hear how you were able to pull off that small miracle. I'll do the same, and we can run away together."

Even as she said it, the hope grew large in her heart, taking flight.

"No." It was a command made by not only a prince, but also a man who knew what he wanted. And he didn't want her. It was obvious in everything about him. His body turned away from her. His eyes peered over the top of her head, cold as steel. His voice, all ice and stone, settled wintery and heavy in her stomach. Her hope froze in place before dropping to the pit of her abdomen and shattering.

"Then what? You really want me to marry your brother?"

He didn't look at her, just nodded curtly as if she were a servant to be dismissed.

"Look at me when I talk to you, Gael, because if you don't look me in the eyes and tell me what you want, I will march back in that room and let everyone know what happened between us, consequences be damned. Unless you tell me you don't love me, that you don't want me for yourself. I have to hear it, Gael."

He turned toward her, slow and intentional wIth each motion of his head, his torso. He didn't soften, didn't release the tension wrapped like a tightly wound coil around each of his limbs.

But he met her gaze.

Despite the frigid waves wafting off his shoulders, the icicles he shot in her direction with his chilly stare, she didn't cower from him. She held her ground, her shoulders, back, and chin high. She'd survived her father's household, for crying out loud. She could match wits with a man her equal.

"I don't love you, Elisabeth."

She cringed at the use of her given name, one only her father and strangers used. To hear it on his lips as he denounced her sliced through her resolve. "I thought we could make a go of it back then, but we've both changed. Even if none of that were true, you have a duty to your country, your family, as do I. What we had, as you so eloquently put it back then in the islands, must remain there." He paused, and she waited for anything, any hint that she'd misheard him, that he'd snap out of his duty-bound coma as she had just moments before and come back to her. "Was that clear enough for you?"

Lissa fought the primal urge to run at him, to pummel

him with her fists to break him out of the icy barricade he hid behind. At the same time, an ache so profound it almost leveled her opened up in her chest. When she'd laid eyes on him in the Great Hall, a rekindled hope for a future she'd dreamt about in the privacy of her deepest thoughts had emerged. Now, it crumbled to her feet like dust on a forgotten road.

She steeled herself, swallowed the pain of rejection like she'd done her whole life, and forced a smile.

"Very well. I'll marry Tomás and live happily ever after. Or something like that. But make no mistake, this is the last I will think of you, address you so informally, or care what happens to you outside of you being my brother-in-law. Once I walk away, it will be forever, Gael."

A flicker of emotion passed over his features, but it disappeared just as quickly, the stony expression settling back on his pursed lips and tight jaw. "That's how it must be, then. Now, if you'll excuse me, I need to attend to my hand. Good day, Princess."

He walked down the hall, away from her, and a small sob bubbled up from her chest. Before it could escape and give away the suffering and agony going on beneath her stoic exterior, she swallowed it back.

The only way for her to survive this was if she followed his lead and detached herself.

From the pain.

From the idea that her life was her own to live.

From him.

She would do just that—heck, she'd been doing it her entire life and had gotten damned good at it if she said so herself. But mark her words, she would forget Gael Reyes ever existed, even if it took the rest of her life to do it.

CHAPTER THREE

Gael paced the floor of the suite he kept in the castle, pausing each time he got to the window overlooking the Cantabrian Sea to the North. It was a majestic view, one replete with oceanside cliffs and white sand beaches that rivaled the Mediterranean to the East. Honestly, though, Gael couldn't care less about beaches, white sand or otherwise. He wouldn't care if his northern view peered out over a slum yard. Because more importantly, he had a direct line of sight into the guest suite where Lissa was supposed to be sleeping to the South.

Except the light was still on and she definitely wasn't sleeping. The shades were drawn, but she paced behind them, casting a long, curvaceous shadow on the white linen. His stomach lurched every time they passed by their windows at the same time, and then, like clockwork, his pants would tighten along the zipper, his body unable to stop thinking about her as anything but his. Especially a certain stubborn part of his anatomy.

A knock on his door was just the distraction he needed. Until he opened it to Lissa's fiancé, his brother.

"Hey there. *Hermano*, that was some drama back there, wasn't it?"

"That's an understatement."

"How's your hand?"

"I'll live." Would he, though? Without her? That remained to be seen, but he wasn't as optimistic as he'd been four hours ago.

"Yeah, I'm sure you will. Why you punched a century-old stone wall is a mystery, though. Care to share?"

"Not really."

"Suit yourself. Anyway, fair warning, Papá's probably on his way down to read you the riot act for the little hand stunt."

"Thanks for the head's up." When Tomás didn't move toward the door, Gael's skin prickled with warning. "What's up?"

Tomás shrugged. "Couldn't sleep. Kept thinking about Elisabeth. She's beyond anything I expected, which, I dunno, changes things."

"What does it change?" Gael uttered through gritted teeth. His stomach clenched like it'd been socked by a prizefighter. He didn't want the answer, wasn't sure he wouldn't repeat what he'd done to the wall with his other hand and his brother's smug face. Not that any of this was Tomás's fault, but still…

"My plans, for one. Do you know I called Nina and told her I can't see her anymore? I mean, what the hell's come over me that I won't entertain the hottest woman in Galicia?"

"You like her, then? Elisabeth?"

Tomás nodded and bit the inside of his cheek, appearing troubled. Well, he wasn't alone.

It was worse than Gael had anticipated. It was one thing that Lissa was here, engaged to his brother, but another thing altogether for Tomás to fall in love with her.

"Well, I'm happy for you, *hermanito*. Love only comes along once in a lifetime and when it does, you're right—it changes everything."

Like your willingness to live without her.

46

"Yeah, I mean, I get it now. Whatever you had with that mystery woman makes sense. I've only been around Elisabeth a few hours, and I'd break the bones of anyone who'd try and hurt her. This is pretty inconvenient, isn't it?"

Tomás chuckled and paced the floor of Gael's suite, but Gael didn't find any of this funny. He gulped back what he wanted to say, swallowing until it nestled deep in his stomach, unable to damn him any more than he was already damned.

"So, what's your plan?"

"I'm not sure. Try and be the man she deserves for starters. Any advice? I figured a sap like you could give a player like me some pointers so I don't eff this up."

Gael considered this. He knew Lissa, not better than anyone, but pretty damn well. He could easily put his needs first and give his brother enough shitty advice that he lost her. But what would Gael have to gain from that? She'd still be married to someone else.

He ran a hand through his hair and bit down on his tongue until the metallic taste of blood filled his mouth. There was only one choice, wasn't there?

"She's amazing. Put her first, *hermanito*. If you do, I have no doubt there won't be a stronger ally than her when you need it most. And don't be shy. Tell her how you feel when you feel it. There's nothing worse than letting the love of your life slip through your fingers because you didn't have the courage to speak up."

Tomás smiled, and something in Gael's chest tightened. For one of them to be happy, the other must suffer. The injustice of it all was going to kill him, he was sure of it.

"Thanks. You have no idea how much this means to me. I knew coming here was a good idea. See you tomorrow for the family brunch? She'll be there, and I want your opinion on whether I have a bleeding pig's chance of winning her over."

Gael mustered the dregs of courage he had on reserve,

but there wasn't much left. Still, it was enough to smile at his brother's honest request. Because if he couldn't have Lissa? He sure as hell wanted her to be happy.

"I wouldn't miss it. Now, go get some rest. You've got your work cut out for you."

Tomás yawned as if on cue, then laughed. "Yeah, I'm beat. But I think I can finally attempt some shut-eye now that I've got that off my chest. You're the best, *hermano.* And don't worry. You'll find that woman you're looking for. Won't it be amazing when we're both paired off and happy?"

Gael let the smile linger until Tomás's head was turned toward the door. When he was safely through it, and the gentle click told him he was alone again, Gael snatched a pillow off the bed and howled into it.

He wouldn't find the woman he was looking for. Clearly, he'd left her, and the promise of a life filled with joy and passion, back in the Kelles. The woman staying unnervingly close to his suite was his brother's fiancée, nothing more.

He glanced at her patio and put a hand to his chest. If only his heart could get on board. The sultry silhouette of his future sister-in-law continued to pace the length of her *terraza*, and his pulse sky-rocketed.

Why wouldn't she just go to bed and leave him at peace?

He opened his phone and looked at one of the two reasons he was still there in Galicia instead of on the first train away from this circus. The royal physician who had taken a look at his hand had recommended scans be done, which, looking at them now, confirmed what the pain shooting up his arm suggested—a clean break in two places. Not counting his heart, of course.

The other reason he couldn't leave had something to do with the near-pint of straight *orujo* he'd self-medicated with. The six-pack of beer he slammed between shots hadn't helped much, either. When he couldn't locate the keys in his pockets or small attaché he'd brought without stumbling headlong down the pebbled path, that was the only sign he needed that a sleepover in the palace was in order.

What he hadn't contended with, however, was the princess as his neighbor.

Like hell, he could fall asleep knowing she was a brisk walk away from his room. Just fifty paces and he could have her in his arms, his skin bared against hers, her fiery mane cascading over him like a waterfall of flames.

Just a few short strides and he could erase the asinine words he'd uttered two hours before. But despite her physical proximity, she'd never been more distant than she was living next door to him. She was promised to his brother, and Gael might be a lot of things, but he wasn't a home-wrecker.

Still, she haunted him. Her body, what she was capable of doing with it, was his brother's gift now. An uninvited and unwanted image of her nude body, lithe and agile atop his brother's, both of them in the throes of passion, hurled itself against the back of Gael's skull. *Dammit.*

He sucked another ounce of *orujo* from the near-empty bottle and coughed half of it back up, cringing at the burn in the back of his throat.

Another harsh rap at the door roused him from his self-imposed prison of circular thinking where Lissa was involved. He shook his head, rubbing the plaster cast the orthopod fitted him with. He wished it hurt half as much as his constricted chest, but that wasn't the case. Proof the body could endure far more than the proverbial heart.

"Dammit, Tomás, you really need to get some—" he started, shutting up when his guest frowned at him with paternal frustration. He should have chugged the rest of the bottle of liquor to fortify himself against this conversation.

"Papá. What are you still doing up? Aren't you usually drunk and passed out this time each night? Or is my watch broken?" He looked down at his cast and giggled, swaying in the process. "Oh, wait. I'm not wearing a watch anymore." He laughed at his own joke, a set of hiccups rattling his chest every few seconds. It wasn't his finest moment, but he was far past caring.

"Are you drunk?" his father asked, stepping into the room and surveying the mess of clothes and empty beer cans on the floor. "Never mind. That much is obvious. And I see Doc Miguel wasn't exaggerating. What were you thinking, Gael? You're an officer of the Royal Navy and you slammed your fist into a wall like a drunken midshipman."

His father looked down at his cast, a scowl twisting his lips. He looked older than Gael remembered. Fatter, too. He could still take him or his brother on without too much of a challenge, but he wasn't the god-like man Gael recalled from growing up. Then again, they were all older, weren't they? Softer in certain places. Gael rubbed his cast, distracted by its cause.

"A door."

"What's that?" his father asked, his tone sharp. Gael may have been as drunk as he'd ever been—since his eighteenth birthday, anyway—but he could recognize his father's annoyance and disappointment in him in a pitch-dark room, at night, with his eyes closed.

"I punched a door, not a wall."

"Son, so help me, I don't understand you sometimes. You're the smartest man I know, but you seem hell-bent on making some rather idiotic decisions."

Gael didn't understand himself much either lately. For instance, he wanted to tell his dad why he was so hung up on a woman he couldn't have. Lady Fortune didn't seem to think they belonged together, so why wasn't he able to let her go? Meeting her that night, he'd thought was destiny in the making. He'd been so certain, so confident.

Ha!

Well, didn't pride always precede the fall? He'd gone

tumbling face-first down a rocky cliff after that night, that was for sure. His father was right—Gael was making some piss-poor choices where Lissa was involved.

Not anymore. From that point on, Lissa was just another person to him. He'd go home, his *real* home on base in Malaga, and work like he'd never worked before until he could make a fire in his hearth and not think of her fiery curls, see the emerald tint of the rolling sea on deployment and not ache for her jade eyes to peer into his.

He hiccupped again, the bird-like chirp loud in the otherwise quiet room.

"Why're you here?" he grumbled, grabbing the bottle of liquor and tilting it back into his open mouth. When only a drop of the lemony liquid touched his tongue, he tossed the empty bottle on the bed, annoyed. Finishing the bottle in a single night, along with the imported chasers he'd consumed as well, was a mistake he'd pay for in the morning. Oh well. It was the distraction from all sorts of other issues he'd needed. And it had helped solidify his plan to forget Elisabeth Oberon.

Curse that he finally knew the wretched woman's name. *A day late...* He giggled again at his unspoken joke.

"Well, I came to address the Captain of the First Squadron, Third Battalion in His Highness's Royal Navy. Will you come find me when he returns and this *chico boracho* is gone?" His father gestured to Gael's shirt with an arrogant flick of his wrist, the former which was stained with his fifth beer that had exploded on him, and rumpled like he'd gone three rounds with a prizefighter. The rest of his body felt like he had, too.

He sighed, straightened his shoulders, and tried to resemble the man his father needed. Anything to not be the weak, broken man living beneath his skin, crying and hopeless.

"I'm right here, Papá. I just needed to numb the pain. It'll pass. What do you need?"

"I have a mission, one that will allow you to stay on

51

light duty with that hand of yours."

Hope kindled the almost-extinguished flame in Gael's chest. "How long? And what kind of mission?"

"Top secret, and for a couple of days or weeks. We won't know for a bit. You'll stay on full duty, though, so the injury won't go on your military record."

Gael considered the freedom a few weeks away from the castle and wedding planning would afford him. Maybe he'd get lucky and he'd miss his brother's wedding altogether.

"I have surgery tomorrow morning, but I'll be out by noon. Six weeks of nothing, then rehab. Will that work?"

His father paused, and Gael regretted asking. He learned a long time ago not to talk someone out of what they were offering him. Especially if it was something he wanted. He could have used that advice when Lissa had literally thrown herself into his arms in the hallway that evening. Dammit.

Please. I'll do anything you ask. Just get me out of here, away from them, from her.

Finally, his father grumbled something Gael couldn't make out in Galician. He looked at Gael, uncertainty in his gaze, but he nodded.

"All right. It's yours. Meet me in my chancery after you're out of surgery. I hope it goes well, son."

Gael nodded, afraid to say anything that might change his father's mind. He needed this as much as he'd needed anything in his life. A chance for a fresh start.

"And Gael," the King called when he got to the door.

"Yes, Papá?"

"Don't screw this up."

Gael smiled. "I won't." He couldn't. It was his last chance to get his life back on track before Lissa got the best of him and dragged him back under her spell. No, he would give this project every last bit of his energy so he never had the chance to make a life-changing decision based on a woman again.

Damn if he didn't disagree the next morning, though. *Oof.* About the energy, anyway.

A bigger mistake than drinking his weight in alcohol last night, especially when his normal consumption consisted of no more than a glass of wine in the evenings, was leaving the drapes open. The light poured in, acting like a laser shot straight to his forehead. The back of his eyes burned and his tongue tasted as if he'd licked the ground in the stables the night before.

He winced. He'd had hangovers before, but this was one of the top five headaches of his life.

Half of it was likely due to the stupid amount of orujo, but the rest was an emotional aftereffect of his interaction with Lissa. Lissa, the siren come back from the deep to claim him. Seeing her again had unhinged something deep within him, letting loose a feral beast with no filter, no conscience, and nothing to lose.

Not just to see her, but to hear her feelings for him, and have to turn her away. It had taken every last bit of strength in him to honor the promises their families had made and not steal away with her in the middle of the night. Another mistake he regretted already.

He wanted her so damned bad, more than the sum of knowing her body, her mind, and then imagining what that would be like again after two years without it. No, the reality was nothing so simple as his imagination had drummed up. It was life changing.

Jesus, he'd known she was lethal when he met her, but he didn't think she'd kill him off in the span of a night. He envisioned a life of mind-bending sex, adventures around the globe, and more challenge and love than he'd ever had. *That would be a way to go.* Not this see-her-marry-someone-else bull. That would put him in an early grave, and not in a fun way.

He shuddered under a piercing stab in his temple amidst the pounding in the rest of his skull. He needed a painkiller, and quick. As he sat up and put his feet on the cool stone floor, he remembered his father coming in the night before.

He'd been drunk, sure, but every word of their conversation came back to him in full color. More than that, the emotional imprint of the discussion came back. He was filled with an underlying hope that there might be a way out of the mess he'd just gotten himself into.

The mission his father had proposed, vague as it was, was his ticket out of there.

Suddenly, he didn't need a pill to solve what ailed him. He needed to get through his surgical appointment so he could find out what that magic ticket entailed. It sounded militaristic in nature, but his father rarely involved himself with matters of state. So, why now?

Hmmm. All the curiosities he had about the mystery gig now that he was sober sent a fire raging through him that burned through the ache in his head.

Whatever it was, he *needed* it.

Three hours later, pins set and hand rebandaged, Gael could barely feel the sting of the surgery or the fatigue from the local anesthetic. He practically ran to his father's office, desperation intermingled with hope pushing out every other emotion he'd accumulated in the past twenty-four hours.

He whistled down the corridor to his father's office, relishing the fact that if he played his cards right, it would be the last time he walked this path for some time. By the time he got back, hopefully Tomás and Lissa would be on their honeymoon and he'd be free of them. Sure that didn't get him through the holidays the following year, nor his overactive imagination where she was concerned, but it was a start.

No matter what, seeing Lissa and his brother together was going to royally suck, but he could put it off for a bit and work through the initial sting.

He got to the ornate wooden door of his father's enormous suite—his office, sitting room, and bedroom all lie beyond that threshold—and knocked with his good hand. A smile erupted on his face as he waited for the familiar command to enter. Hell, he didn't even have a headache anymore. This was exactly what he needed, to be back to work. It had been two years since he'd been able to concentrate fully on a mission without working side jobs to track Lissa down, without wondering where she was, who she was with, thoughts of whether she was thinking of him too pulling his focus. Now, he could give himself over to whatever the detail demanded and feel okay about leaving her behind. For good.

"Come in," his father's voice boomed. Only that man could send any shred of warmth and joy running for the hills. Still, nothing could dampen Gael's spirit. Not even his old man and his stubborn refusal to admit feelings other than those that ran his country's business.

It took Gael a moment to adjust to the dim light in the room, and then another to regain his breath as he took in the small crowd in the office. His brother stood immediately inside the entrance, his usual light demeanor stripped from his colorless face.

Gael looked back at his father, whose somber brows tucked in neatly above his nose. His pursed lips drawn tight looked a mite more serious than normal as well.

Who died?

Then, as his gaze made its way back to his brother, he caught something he'd missed on his first pass through the room. How he'd overlooked the orange-red flames atop creamy skin was beyond the scope of his imagination, but there she was nonetheless.

Her hair was pulled over one shoulder, exposing her skin where her fitted turtleneck tank didn't cover her. Gael clenched his fists so tightly together to keep the impulse to touch her at bay that when he released them momentarily, small half-moon circles remained embedded in his palms. Her eyes shone up at him, and he was only able to relax when she smiled weakly in his direction. His head pounded again, but not because of the obscene amount of booze he'd imbibed the night before. Just seeing her sent all his senses into overdrive, and he was barely operating at half-tilt today.

Jesus. So much for forgetting all about Elisabeth Oberon. He was as much at the mercy of her whims as he was two years ago, two months ago, two days ago. Not a damn thing had changed, had it? He sighed, and then the crippling realization of why they were all in the room together slapped him out of his Lissa-induced walking coma.

They knew. Somehow, it had gotten out about his affair with the betrothed princess, meaning their geese were cooked. Or worse. That was the only explanation for the small council sitting on the King's overstuffed desk chairs, staring warily up at Gael.

He opened his mouth to protest, to take the fall for her and explain the situation.

They didn't know who the other was. It was two years ago.

He'd walked away the moment he discovered who she was and who she was supposed to marry.

None of it would matter, of course, but he had to try, had to do something to keep the union intact. He would *not* be responsible for ruining his brother's life just because he'd self-sabotaged his own.

Lissa shook her head, a subtle gesture meant only for him. It kept him on alert but silent. She cleared her throat before addressing the room. "Well, now that we are all here, shall we get started?"

His father nodded his approval and gestured to her to continue.

Wait. The King was deferring to the future queen, a guest in their home, in a private, family meeting? One where Gael was supposed to be given top-secret military orders? His skin pricked with warning, but he couldn't fathom what it all meant. Not yet. His only hope was that it wasn't what his first intuition told him—his father knew about him and Lissa.

Time, and the rising pitch of his father's voice and eyebrows, would tell him if he was right. Only, he wouldn't see the right hook until it hit him across the jaw. His brother's presence there was as worrisome as seeing Lissa in his father's royal chambers.

"Señor Ryes—pardon me, *Capitán* Reyes—I came to your father with an urgent matter I hoped you could help with."

She gazed up at him through thick, copper lashes that fluttered on his heart every time she blinked. It was her who came to the King? Nothing except his father offering to give Gael a foot massage would have surprised him more. He switched tacks as fast as he could without giving away anything.

"Of course, Lady Oberon. How can I assist you? Papá?"

She smiled, the dimple on her left cheek tilting her grin just off center. He moved his legs to hide what was an ardent appreciation of her body. One that had no place in the King's quarters surrounded by her future husband and father-in-law.

Good God, why was she there? Tempting him within an inch of his life. He set his gaze on the King, a decidedly less-distracting glance than Lissa's.

"The Princess has received a threat, Gael. It is obviously time sensitive as the miscreant who sent her the letter knows of her whereabouts. It was received last night on the front steps outside her suite."

The front steps of the guest suite? Inside the palace? It was impossible, and yet, the proof hit his good hand moments later.

The King handed over a crumpled sheet of paper, an amalgamation of letters sliced from other publications to spell out a nasty threat to Lissa. Gael felt like he'd been punched. Someone had dared threaten the woman he loved? On *his* land, in *his* home? Fire raged in his veins, hot and liquid.

"You were threatened *here*?" He wheeled on her, fists raised until he caught the wayward glance of his brother, confusion etched on his features. Gael's pulse spiked, and he tried to reclaim the breath that had somehow left his body. It was a futile attempt since another crippling realization hit him square across the chest, making sure any oxygen stayed far from his lungs.

Lissa wasn't his to defend, to save. She never had been and never would be. He recovered as quickly as he could outwardly, but inside, he was at war.

"I'm sorry, but this is an outrage. On behalf of our country, I apologize that you're in this position. What can I do?" He turned back to his father, his heart burning as if it had been scorched over an open flame.

"Well, we need to get the princess to a place she's safe until this threat is discovered and dealt with. We can't very well send her home to Aldonia if there is any question of her health and safety."

"Where are your parents?" he asked, their absence suddenly as visceral as if they'd brushed up against his suit jacket. His heart sank when her gaze fell to the floor along with her smile.

"They've gone home until the wedding. They've got so much to prepare, and all."

The rest of the room nodded in agreement, but Gael saw right past her dismissal of their inexcusable actions. They just dropped her off to be married—to a stranger no less—and then never looked back? So, they were safe at home in their own suites, and Lissa was in a foreign country, about to wed a stranger, her life at risk. Shame on them. They'd probably only come back for the wedding because they'd be acting on ceremony, not because of any lasting affection for their daughter. She'd alluded to their overbearing ways in the Islands, but he hadn't known who she was so his perspective had been off-tilt. Now, in the light of who she was and what they were asking of her, it was crap, all of it.

"I understand," he lied. How was he supposed to agree with parents discarding their child after she'd given up everything for them? He did, however, comprehend on a cellular level how disappointing family could be, and his only hope was that sentiment would come through in his words. He turned back to his father. "Perhaps the country house by the Cantabrian? No one knows it's still in the family and it's not registered on any city plans since it's a royal property. And while you get her out of here—now, if you can spare the manpower—I can spearhead the recon for the guy who thinks he can get away with this on our turf—"

"Whoa, there, son. Hold on a minute. I appreciate your enthusiasm, but your role will be to escort Lady Oberon to the Cantabrian property and await there until you've heard that the threat has been neutralized. You won't have any contact with us until then so communication can't be traced, but I trust your military training will make sure you have everything you need from the country before you depart. Three decoy transports will be sent at the same time to distract from your exit with the princess, who will both travel disguised as farmers from the region."

His father continued with an elaboration of the transport and mission details, but Gael heard him as if he were speaking from underwater. All his thoughts, energy, and focus were on his father's assignment for him.

He was a trained military officer and he'd been relegated to babysitting duty.

Not only that, the mission that was supposed to take him as far from the Princess as possible so he could begin the painstaking and arduous journey to getting over her had accomplished the exact opposite. Instead, he'd be shacked up with her in a romantic beach house, with nothing but time and memories of their affair to keep them company.

It was a suicide mission.

He loved her, dammit, and being alone with her would be an exquisite torture he wasn't sure he'd survive. And to be forced to walk the property each night, alert and aware of any changes in his surroundings to keep her safe? It would be impossible with her sleeping just feet from him. Look how well that situation had gone last night. Someone had sneaked past their defenses and left a note at their door—*their damned door!*—while an inebriated Gael lay passed out on his bed.

Jesus, this was a mess. A mess he saw no way out of, not if they expected to keep their affair two years ago a secret.

His father shook his hand, walking out of the room in deep conversation with Tomás, leaving him alone with his charge. *That was it?* He'd missed the bigger points of the plan, but he got the gist—he was Lissa's bodyguard for at least the next two weeks. She was still off-limits, but meanwhile, he had no accountability other than to keep her safe. Not a good plan when all he wanted to do was tear her clothes off and ravage her from her crimson hair to her cherry-red-polished toes. His skin prickled with the realization that everything he'd wanted the past two years was being handed to him on a silver platter.

He and Lissa alone on a deserted beach, no one around or there to intrude.

Only the context of the trip soured that thought as soon as it entered his mind. He couldn't touch her, couldn't kiss her, and hell, he probably shouldn't talk to her outside of the mission. It was shaping up to be the worst assignment he'd ever had, and that included transporting an American pop icon to Barcelona the year prior. The poor girl had indulged in far too many *tapas* and *rioja*, only to lose the contents of her stomach on national television just before her concert. That hot mess of an assignment would be a cakewalk compared to the task set before him now.

He ran his hands through his hair, trying not to notice Lissa's eyes that seemed intent on finding his. One look from her and his resolve would diminish to dust, leaving them both exposed and vulnerable. If they were caught by his father, they'd wish for a threat on their lives he would make their existence so miserable.

Still, he felt her in all the places she'd branded him with her lips, her delicate fingertips. Each inch of his skin touched by hers burned with recognition. He needed some air, and fast.

"Your Grace, I've got to go see about our departure plans. I suggest you pack as quickly as possible. I doubt we will remain at the palace longer than an hour. Wait for me to retrieve you in your suite, and do not answer the door for anyone other than me. Is that clear?"

"You aren't going to walk me to my room to make sure I'm safe?" There was a rough edge to her voice, but beneath it, he sensed her fear. He almost cracked, almost scooped her up in his arms and never let her go. All he wanted was her safety and happiness. But he wasn't the man to give her either. That privilege had been stripped from him when he gave up all his responsibilities for her two years ago. His role was temporary, and like before, would evaporate the moment they left the beach.

"I'm not," he said, only half turning to face her. He didn't trust his body not to mutiny and wrap her up in an embrace before his mind could talk him out of it. "I'll have my right-hand man accompany you and stand outside your door until I can find you. Will that be acceptable?"

From the cover of his vision, he caught her nod and sighed. Just before he could leave the same way his father and brother had just moments before, a hand on his arm stopped him.

A sharp jab of pain as his chest seized almost felled him. Her touch held so much power over him, it was as if he didn't have a dress shirt and suit jacket on. How he wanted to wheel around and press his lips to hers, the consequences be damned.

He held back, though, his teeth gritted to the point of pain searing his jaw, only turning his head to meet her gaze.

She'd closed the millimeters between them, her scent swirling around his face, intoxicating him. When she leaned her head against his shoulder, he couldn't breathe for fear of taking too much of her in, never being rid of her. His stomach clenched as he fought the desire to shift his shoulders and let her collapse into his strength.

But that would be impossible. He'd made sure of that when he'd turned down his responsibility to Galicia, to Spain.

"Yes, Your Grace?" he asked through pursed lips. Why couldn't she see that her closeness was killing him? The look on her face wasn't light and pleasant, either. Her cheeks were burnished nearly as red as her hair, but her lips were drawn and white as if masking a great pain.

"Gael," she said, using his first name and completely disarming him, "I'm glad it's you. I feel safer knowing you'll be with me, protecting me."

He froze, not sure what to say. He should have felt better at hearing that, but the softness of her voice, the fear lacing her words? It sent a wave of frustration coursing through his limbs. He nodded and stepped away from her.

Then, without a word, he walked out, leaving her alone in the bare, cold room, wishing things were different, wishing he'd been more patient so he could be the one to protect her after the culprit had been caught. He wanted the forever job of being by her side, not the temporary assignment.

If he ever found the person responsible for putting him in this situation, tasked to guard the woman he loved to keep her safe for her husband—his brother—he'd kill them with his bare hands.

Because he might be there to protect her life, but who

was going to make sure his heart was safe from her?

CHAPTER FOUR

Lissa stood on the tile patio of the master suite overlooking the Cantabrian Sea, her heart at a fragile sort of peace for the first time in two years. The azure water raced up to kiss the pale-pink sand before sliding softly away, leaving only a thin line of shells to mark its passage. On the horizon, the sun had come up a bright orange, tinting the light sheen of clouds above her the same color. Warmth enveloped her bare shoulders, despite the fact that it was winter everywhere else in Europe. How could Christmas be so close when the only clothes that felt comfortable were a bathing suit and sundress?

She stretched her arms out, letting the heat tickle her skin while it was still early. Later in the day, she'd have to hide under a shade again, but for the time being, she relished the warmth.

What was it about the sea that was so familiar, so calming? When things had come to a head with her parents two years ago, she'd sprinted to the furthest body of water she could find a flight to, in need of both distance and salt water to heal.

She'd found both, sure, but also so much more than that. She'd happened upon a man who fulfilled her physical desires while creating and satisfying countless more. Not only that, but he saw through to her core, to the person she wanted to be, and dragged that forgotten woman to the surface.

And now that same man threatened to undo her.

Gael.

She sighed and focused her gaze on the small sailboat heading along the coastline toward San Sebastián.

She hadn't so much as clapped eyes on the man sworn to protect her since they'd arrived three days ago. Not that she hadn't tried to pin him down and confront his obvious discomfort around her. Because there wasn't a cell in her body that believed he didn't still care for her. He'd searched for her the whole two years they'd been separated, and the kiss they'd shared back at the palace? It spoke of all the words he couldn't, or wouldn't, say.

She ran her fingers over her lips, recalling the electricity that had seared her skin that night, reminding her of all she'd found—and lost—when she'd left the Kelles Islands, and Gael in the process.

This morning, she'd risen before the sun, intent on finding Gael, even if she had to do so by pouncing on him when he wasn't expecting her. She finished watching the sunrise—her favorite part of each day, when the world stretched before her with promise—then tiptoed to the set of double doors that separated their suites. Smiling at her ingenious idea to catch him off guard, she flung them open, only to find his bed made and not a sign that he'd been there at all the night before.

Where the hell was he?

She was about to head back into her room to don the bathing suit, hat, and book trio she'd survived the last three days of exile with, but she stopped. He didn't have any right to treat her like an afterthought. Sure, he had his staff—only one woman who'd been with the family for over forty years—help her with food, or any of her other needs, but she didn't want that.

She wanted *him*.

She stomped over to his office, no longer concerned about subtlety. He thought he could hide from her? Well, he had another thing coming. She jiggled the doorknob, not bothering to knock. Why should she stand on ceremony when he hadn't checked in on her wellbeing even once?

The door was locked, but his voice snuck under the gap between the door and stone flooring, low and serious, so at least he was still there in the house. She pressed her ear to the thick oak, hoping to hear what was so important it required discussing behind a barricaded door, but she only caught snippets of the one-sided conversation.

It was enough to deduce that Gael was hell-bent on single-handedly tracking down the criminal who'd broken into the palace and threatened her. So, that was his plan? Avoid talking to her, being around her, and use protecting her as an excuse? It was thin at best. At worst, it would be a long two weeks if this kept up.

Besides, his father had specifically told Gael he was to leave the sleuthing to them.

That was it. She'd lost any shred of patience with the man. He was as infuriating and stubborn as her father, albeit without the evil streak.

She rapped on the door, loud and persistent. *Let him ignore me now*. Finally, just when she was about to resort to using her foot to kick the thick wood and save her hand from the fate Gael had endured back at the palace, the door flung open, an enraged Gael on the other side of it.

She bit her tongue to prevent the gasp that had snuck up her throat from escaping.

He looked like Hell had taken him hostage for a month straight. His hair stood on end where it met his forehead, as if he'd consistently grasped it in frustration. His previously smooth jawline was raked with coarse, dark stubble, and his eyes were a dark gray-blue like the sea after a storm.

Her stomach lurched and heat spread from her center through her limbs. Christ. He'd captivated her with his incriminatingly good looks when they'd first met and stunned her silent with how much he'd grown into himself in the two years since that first meeting when she'd seen him again at the palace. But now? How was he still so spectacularly handsome when his polish, his shine had worn off, leaving a disheveled but devastatingly gorgeous man in its place?

Curse him for maintaining his raw sexuality when he was flustered, unlike her, who typically resembled a frightened meerkat just pulled from the river.

"What?" he barked out, his eyes feral, wild. When they focused on hers, they softened, but his lips remained pressed tight. "What do you need, Elisabeth?"

Elisabeth? Okay, he'd taken this pretending-they-didn't-know-each-other thing too far. That one word snapped her out of her trepidation. She straightened her shoulders and tossed her hair back over her shoulder before placing her hands on her hips. Two could play at this game.

"I need to speak with you, Gael."

He opened his mouth to reply, an excuse evident in his furrowed brow.

"*Now.*" She turned on her heels and stalked down the corridor toward the back patio. Gael looked like he hadn't seen anything other than the fluorescent lights in his office for days. Sunshine would do them both a world of good. His heavy footsteps echoed against the walls behind her.

Good. He was following her.

When she pushed through the curtains leading out to the balcony, the sun hit her with a blast of heat, warming her skin and calming her racing heart. She faced the sea, the Atlantic Ocean beyond her scope but offering a world of possibility. Even though her eyes weren't on the silk drapes acting as a loose barrier between the sitting room and patio, she felt the moment he appeared behind her.

Despite the heat, her skin prickled with chills from the

air brushing against her. Her stomach flipped and sent a blast of warmth to the secret spot that had ached for him every night the past two years.

She turned slowly, needing to take in his appearance in pieces so as not to overwhelm her senses. Though he still looked as disheveled as he did before, his shirt untucked and tie loosened around his neck, his jaw had relaxed, his eyes a light blue again, indicating whatever storm he'd been struggling against had passed, for now anyway.

Her heart beat loud against her ribcage, echoing in her ears.

She swallowed back a wave of lust that couldn't be part of this conversation. They needed to talk, not jump each other, especially since the latter was what had gotten them into this mess in the first place.

"What do you want to talk about?" he asked. It came out gruff, a demand as he was likely accustomed to making. Well, not of her. She wasn't his underling, nor his subordinate, and she refused to be talked to as such, especially when she hadn't done anything to warrant it.

"Gael, do I really deserve that tone from you? Please tell me how any of this is my fault."

He raised his injured hand wrapped in an athletic brace and pushed his fingers through his hair, just as she'd imagined him doing in the solitude of his office.

"I'm sorry. I didn't ask for this either, Liss. In fact, I explicitly wanted anything but this."

She bristled under the flippant dismissal and choked back the hurt that rose up her throat like bile.

"Well, I'm sorry my life and safety have caused you such an inconvenience. I'll leave you to your work." She turned to go. She'd tried to reach him, but he clearly didn't appreciate the effort. She'd just ride out the rest of the trip on the beach, working on her reading list and avoiding an inevitable sunburn as long as possible. At least here she was free of her parents, free of her obligations. But she'd never be free of him.

She only made it two steps before his hand settled firm on her bare forearm, scorching her with his heat.

"Lissa, I didn't mean it like that. Jesus, I can't do anything right, can I?"

The defeat slipped out along with the words, slicing through her heart like a warm blade. What could she possibly say to that? She felt the way she felt, and he obviously didn't feel the same.

"I don't know how to be around you, Lissa. I'm sorry, I didn't mean to ignore you, but every time I'm around you, I want to go back to how we were *there*. You see how that might be problematic considering why we're here. So, I figured I'd try to at least help track down whoever's after you. You know, two birds, one stone."

She smiled. So, he did feel the same. That was at least something, even if he didn't believe they could do anything about it. She'd make it her sole mission from that moment forward to prove him wrong.

"I don't agree. We're here, together, alone. Don't you think it's the perfect situation for us to explore our feelings for each other?" She ran a hand along the outline of his shoulder and trailed it along his bicep until she reached his hand. She took it in hers and squeezed, feeling the flames between their touch ignite. It had always been this way with him. How could they ignore that?

He wrenched his hand free and punched the air in front of him with his good hand.

"That's not possible. You get under my skin, Liss, to the point I can't concentrate on anything else. And somehow we're here. Like fate hasn't had enough of a go of us. No, now we're stuck in a house on the beach while your future husband—not me, may I remind you, since I was a total jerk who abdicated his throne and right to your hand—tracks down a killer who wants you dead. Perfect isn't a word I'd use to describe this."

A surge of guilt washed over Lissa. Her smile faltered. "Um, do you know why you were chosen? For this detail, I mean?" Why her voice had to give her away by rising an octave she considered a personal travesty.

"I don't know why they asked me. There are a thousand officers who can handle embassy duty, which this is, more or less. It's so far below my skill level I don't know how I made the list, even with my injured hand. I should be out there helping them catch the SOB who's doing this to you. But don't worry. I won't let anything happen to you, Lissa. I'm damn good at what I do, so you'll be safe here with me until I can deliver you to your fiancé."

He spat that last word like venom.

He took a tentative step toward her, but she could see what it cost him. His hands trembled the closer he got to her.

"I know I'm safe, Gael."

She paused, unsure of how much more to share that wouldn't add to his stress. When she'd heard of the threat, her parents on the road nearly two hours by then, she'd felt empty, more frightened than she'd ever been in her life. The only reason she calmed and gathered her wits that morning was knowing she'd be safe with Gael. Gael, the man she loved, the man she was *supposed* to marry, if he hadn't been so foolhardy as to renounce his birthright.

Oh well. At least they had this time together. It wasn't much, not even a drop of what she truly desired, but she'd take what she could get while she could get it. She would never admit it aloud, but as scared as she was about the validity of the note sent to unnerve her—someone had penetrated the castle security to deliver it personally—she was grateful for the excuse to spend the next two weeks or more with Gael. Alone. On a private beach. It would be romantic if it weren't so damned petrifying.

That being said, she owed him the truth about why he was there at least.

"Gael, I have to tell you something."

He raised his gaze to meet hers, and the electric charge

that had sparked at their touch passed between them again.

She inhaled deeply, her chest trembling with nerves. "I, um, I asked for you, specifically. I wanted you to be my protector, not some stranger. You have to admit, it's a bit strange this all happened, giving us a way to spend time together." She smiled, hoping it would be enough to melt the chill that iced over the once-hot connection binding them.

"You *what*? Oh, Lissa, *please* tell me that's not true. It would be insane." He growled, not as feral a sound as he'd made the night he broke his hand, but in the same, pained vein.

Okay. Or not.

"Perhaps, but it doesn't matter. You are the only one I feel safe with, Gael. Our time in the islands wasn't just a weekend for me, which is a big deal since I don't do relationships. And you already admitted it was more to you, too. Aren't you grateful we get the time to figure that out?"

"Wait. So when the threat emerged, you asked for *me* to escort you? When I told you I didn't think it was a good idea for us to be around each other? Never mind, you're past crazy. You should be committed."

He was pacing now, striding with militant purpose across her balcony. She took off after him, her hands balled into fists. Why was he being so damned difficult?

"Gael, I'm not marrying your brother. Not even if you don't love me. I know I said I could, but last night I had time to think, and there's no way. My parents will be furious, of course, but I can't tie myself to another when my heart is taken by someone else. You walked away from your ordained future once, and you survived. I'm doing the same thing when we get back."

He stared at her as if she'd grown three heads. Couldn't he hear her? She loved him, and only him. How could he expect her to marry his brother when he felt the same way about her? A stranger, perhaps, if it meant the difference between life and death for her country, but a social climb for her parents tying her to the kin of the man who'd crept into her life and heart two years ago, a man she'd never forgotten? Impossible.

"It doesn't matter what your reasons were. They'll find out about us, and we'll be dead. Not figuratively, either. This is treason, and now I've broken the law as a prince and member of the Royal Navy. My head'll be put on a spit to warn off anyone else who might have aspirations to pull a stupid stunt like this in the future."

"So what?"

He wheeled around as if to scold her, only to run smack into her chest with his own. She stumbled backward but didn't falter. His forehead was lined with crevasses and valleys miles deep, but beyond that, he looked defeated, exhausted. All she wanted was to take him in her arms and love him back to life.

"So *what?* Listen, Lissa, just because you've lost your mind doesn't mean all of us are just going to follow suit. What do you think is going to happen here if we indulge in our feelings for each other? It doesn't change the fact that we still have to fly back into the hornet's nest when we're done."

"I don't care. I love you, and I want to be with you, Gael. No matter the cost."

His brow furrowed again, and the storm in his eyes returned, casting a shadow over the rest of his features.

"You…" he trailed off, pacing in front of her where he could keep an eye on her now. "You didn't write the note, did you?"

Lissa didn't realize she was walking until she was in front of him again, her hand and pointer finger wagging in his face. Blood rushed to her cheeks, setting each word she uttered on fire.

"Now who's crazy? How could you ever, *ever* assume I would do anything so reckless and foolish? I love you, Gael, and I want to find a way to spend our lives together at *almost* any cost. But something that deceptive, not to mention illegal? Never. I'll find a way for it to work between us the right way. Do you understand me?"

Her breath came in ragged gulps as she tried to contain her rage. How dare he accuse her of such duplicity? Maybe she didn't know him as well as she thought she did. He certainly didn't know her, or what she was and wasn't capable of.

"I'm sorry, Liss. I had to ask, though." He took her hand in his, closing her extended finger into his palm. He pulled her close, and the rage turned instantly to desire. He was like a magician, the way he could morph her feelings at will. "What were you thinking asking for me to take care of you here? Don't you understand how hard it is to be around you and not take you straight to my bed to make you forget all about any man other than me?"

His voice had softened, though, and she swallowed back a victory squeal. She'd broken through.

She grinned, and he growled something at her in a language she didn't understand, though his smile remained pinned to her along with his gaze. Lord, was he sexy when he did that. But she'd won. She'd get the man into her bed and let her body do the rest of the talking. Then, if he still didn't want her, she'd figure out a way to get them both out of this unscathed. But that wasn't plan A.

Plan A was getting him to love her back. She reached up and pressed her lips to his, opening his mouth with her tongue.

And it started now.

CHAPTER FIVE

Gael shouldn't have been surprised at how their bodies melded together, two pieces to the same puzzle that only fit together. Yet, the moment he'd kissed her back at the palace—or when she'd kissed him, rather—he'd been shocked with the renewed realization that there would never be another woman for him. It wasn't only an island romance as his father had insinuated, destined to fade away as soon as the azure horizon did, nor was it the burning need each of them had to escape their respective lives for a moment in time.

No, they fit because they were meant to. Fate sure may have had a funny way of bringing them together, but for the first time since she'd shown up in front of him at the palace, he was glad she was there.

Maybe *glad* wasn't the exact word he was looking for. Exalted, maybe? Euphoric? Scared as hell?

However, as her hand slid up the front of his tousled dress shirt and paused on his chest just above his heart, he stopped trying to find a better word and just succumbed to the bliss that was Lissa's body against his.

Her hands were cool to his overheated skin, but at the same time, her touch fanned a flame that threatened to consume him from the inside out. It was dizzying, the juxtaposition. In a similar conundrum, his head warred with his heart and body, who had teamed up against the former. It begged him to stop, to talk some sense into her, but then her fingers slid underneath the waist of his slacks and he shut his brain off for good. There was no place for his overthinking here.

Hell, there wasn't room for thinking, period.

"You feel good," she whispered against his neck, craning up to slide her tongue along his earlobe. The heat sent him into a tailspin, his slacks suddenly too tight around his zipper.

He ached for more, for her to speed up as much as he wanted to slow down and appreciate every moment he had with her. Every inch of her, every single emotion she drew out of him was a lesson in opposites, and it drove him wild with lust, and more.

"So do you," he spoke into her hair, tangling his fingers in the crimson waves.

He used the thick handfuls of spun copper to pull back her head as gently as he could, exposing her neck so he could kiss her supple, creamy skin. God, she tasted as delectable as she looked, like cherry preserves on vanilla ice cream. The hint of salt from the ocean air added a savory bite to her sweetness, another contrast that awoke a feral drive in him to seek out more of what made her so unique, so perfect, so *Lissa*.

"Take me here, under the sunlight, Gael. Like you did on our first morning together." Her voice was a match, igniting him with a single stroke. How could he possibly deny her when she'd given him everything in a single kiss?

Cradling her shoulders with one arm, and scooping the other underneath her legs, he lifted her into his arms before setting her down softly on the outdoor chaise. Her creamy skin spanned the length of the lounge, and the only things stopping him from exploring every inch of the territory he still knew by heart were a thin swathe of fabric covering her breasts and stomach and a smaller one over the part of her he longed to touch, taste, and claim as he had two years ago.

Keeping her gaze, he started at her hips, his hands steady despite his shaky nerves. This was everything he'd wanted for so long now, and he didn't want to screw it up. Sliding his hands along the curve of her stomach, he paused only to cup her breasts, bare beneath the night shirt she wore.

The soft purr that escaped Lissa's parted lips was all the invitation he needed to continue. He teased her nipples into peaks rivaling the Pyrenees, then lifted her shirt over her head and tossed it aside. Before he tasted the alabaster tips and valleys that had ruled his cravings for two years, he took a moment to appreciate the view before him.

The woman of his dreams lay spread beneath him, supple and open for his pleasure. Behind her, the cerulean waters of his childhood lapped at the private shores that held so many other pleasant memories for him. The scene was something he might have dreamt up if he had the capacity to imagine such perfection.

"Why'd you stop, Capitán?" she asked. The light laugh that punctuated her question snapped him out of his ardent gratitude for the woman and brought him back to her corporeal form.

"Just needed a moment to give thanks for this," he said, dipping his head and pressing his lips to her belly button. She giggled, but when he moved up her body, to the place where her breasts met her taut stomach, the giggle turned to a breathy gasp, urging him on. "And this," he said, kissing the bottom of her breast. She purred, and he trailed his tongue along the curve of her flesh until he found the diamond-hard nipples he'd longed to taste.

"And I couldn't leave this out," he added, blowing cool air on the trail of moisture he'd traced up her body.

"Gael, *please*," she begged. That was all the invitation he needed to shed his clothing and the scant remaining piece of hers and drive into her, giving her everything he had.

If he had any remaining doubts about making love to a woman betrothed to his brother, they had the decency to stay locked tight in his brain while his heart and body went to work loving Lissa in every way they could. Every thrust, every kiss, every embrace seemed both long overdue and as if no time had passed at all since they'd done the same thing in the Kelles.

Always a juxtaposition, this one. Not that he minded. The yin and yang kept him balanced between her edges and he didn't want to be anywhere else.

After hours of giving and taking from each other, she collapsed against him, stroking his bare chest absently.

"Well, that was fun," she teased, kissing his chest. A shiver raced across his skin, cooling it down after hours of exertion under the harsh winter sun. At least the past hour found them under the shade of the cabana once the sun moved past them toward the open ocean.

"I'd argue it's a better way to start the day than I'd originally planned. Thank you for bringing back the joy to this place."

"Was this house ever not happy? I mean, how can you beat this view?"

That was the million-dollar question, wasn't it? Yes, it had held many of the memories he recalled most fondly, but the loss of those—namely the energetic and joy-filled Christmases with his grandparents that stopped when his grandfather passed away—left a gaping hole in Gael's chest. There was no way his parents would ever have put their own anger toward each other aside long enough for them to enjoy a holiday without the grandparents there to tamper the flames, so the last year his grandfather was alive—Gael's eighteenth birthday—was the last year they'd spent at the beach house as a family.

When Gael was an adult, he'd gone there whenever he'd needed a break, but never with anyone else. In fact, he should have been there the year he met Lissa, but his father had taken up temporary residence in the Cantabrian house after a particularly gruesome fight with Gael's mom over a loose-lipped barmaid from town. So, Gael had looked up the furthest locale from his palace and flown there. The Kelles Islands, the second most remote island chain on Earth.

Where he'd met Lissa. The rest, as his brother was fond of saying, was history. It was the future he was more concerned about, but even those pressing worries weren't enough to steal the exultation he'd rediscovered in Lissa.

Sharing the intimate space with her was far more pleasant than he imagined. She somehow kept all the less-than-fun memories at bay and gave him hope that the space, like his life, could be happy once again, so long as she was in it.

He decided to give her a diluted version of the beach house's past so he didn't ruin the mood. "It was a very happy place until we lost my grandfather. After that, it was never the same relaxing vacation home. Until you, that is." He kissed her softly, eliciting a purr of pleasure.

She traced his skin with soft curves and swirls of her finger, leaving a trail of goosepimples in her wake.

"I'm sorry about that. So, if you were looking to relax, what is it you were doing locked up the past three days anyhow? Besides avoiding me, that is."

He sighed. How could he possibly explain how much she drew him to her, how the locked office wasn't to keep her out, but him inside, where he couldn't screw anything up?

So much for that. He kissed the tips of her fingers, wrapped his hand around hers, and squeezed.

"I needed to make you safe," he said, as much to himself as to her. He bent his head down and pressed his lips to her forehead. He'd never get sick of her skin against his, her taste on his lips. Of that, he was certain.

"This is all I need, Gael. I've always felt safe with you. Don't you get that?"

"I do. But I needed to play a part in tracking down the *culo* who thought he could threaten you on my land, in my home. And, well, I thought it was a better way to spend my time than pining after you. One look at you in that metallic bikini and I locked my libido up behind those oak doors so I wouldn't do anything as foolish as this," he said, sliding his hand along her backside, cupping it.

"Or this," he added, bringing his other hand up to her chin and tipping it up. He met her halfway, kissing her softly at first, then as a hunger welled up inside him, with more passion. She matched it with her own, and before he could think too much about how it had happened, she was straddling his hips, taking him inside her again. Another part of loving her he'd never tire of. How his body found the ability to recuperate so quickly under her expert touch was a mystery he'd never figure out.

But why try when the doing was far more fun than the thinking?

Another hour lay behind them, and somehow, they hadn't moved more than flipping positions on the chaise lounge chair.

"Whew," she sighed, sitting up with his head resting on her stomach. "Please tell me why you were hiding away from that. I think it's a perfectly fine way to not only start a morning, but ease our way into the afternoon."

Her stomach grumbled against his ear and he laughed. "I agree, but we need to get some food in you if we want to try to make it to the evening like this."

"I'm not complaining about either. What shall I make? Anything you want after that performance."

He blushed, but then thought about what she'd said.

"You cook?" he asked, feeling bad about the shock that crept into his voice.

He didn't know a royal member of his family who did anything more than demand food be brought to them, with specifics about how and where. He'd bet his inheritance his brother hadn't so much as made a bowl of cereal himself in his sheltered life.

Heck, Gael had only started taking care of himself, meals and all, when he'd moved south for the military. There, they didn't have servants or house staff to attend to his every need. It was actually a blessing, the way he saw it. The more he learned to do on his own, the less beholden he was to other people. That didn't mean he wasn't surprised the princess knew her way around a kitchen.

All the more reason to love her, not that he needed another one.

"You seem surprised. But yes, it was a necessity around our home. My parents couldn't be bothered, and they could never keep a staff longer than a week or two. Most likely because they partied away any funds they needed to maintain that particular part of palace life."

"What do you mean?" he asked, his interest piqued. He'd known she was running from her life two years ago but hadn't known why. Truthfully, they hadn't done much talking back then, something he sorely regretted now.

She ran her fingers through his hair and took a deep breath in. "My parents haven't exactly been the responsible side of the Aldonian family tree. They've pretty much squandered every cent and every opportunity my cousin Robert gave them. So, he cut them off, meaning they had to resort to... less traditional means of sustaining the life they've become accustomed to. Which is why you found me two years ago, drowning my sorrows on a faraway beach with a handsome stranger and a bottle of rum."

She laughed, but it was an empty sound that spoke volumes about the hurt she'd carried with her since then. And for who knows how long before that. An urge to protect her welled up inside his chest again, cutting off his breath. He sat up next to her and pulled her into his arms.

"Is that why they've pawned you off? To make up for their mistakes?"

She nodded against his shoulder, and the protectiveness inside his chest swirled angrily as it mixed with rage at all she'd faced, all that kept them both from getting what they wanted. She deserved better, the best actually. She deserved to be loved and cherished, not shoved into a marriage of stunted convenience that would only actually be convenient for the two people who were supposed to provide her with the world, not wait for her to procure it for them.

Anger simmered below his skin, heating it. "How dare they? Do they really think they'll get anything from you when you marry Tomás?"

She shrugged. "I'm not sure, but it's their only play. They're scrappy and aren't above using every means available to them to get what they want." She paused, her eyes downcast. "I'm sorry, Gael. I don't mean to dampen the mood. I rather liked where our day was heading before they came up. What do you say we put that lunch on hold and pick up where we left off?" She put a hand over the thin towel covering his waist, and the part of him that had been overworked that morning sprang to attention as if it hadn't done a thing.

"That sounds good, but we know that'll keep. Hell, we know it'll do more than keep. I, for one, think we do that particular thing very well and can't wait to practice even more. But, I want to know more about you, Liss. We hardly got a chance to get to know much about each other the last time we were under the same roof. Or swimming in the same ocean. Or wherever else we didn't talk."

A flash of red splashed her cheeks.

"We didn't, did we? Well, what do you want to know?"

He smiled. Okay, they could do this. The talking thing, that was.

"Let's start simple. Do you have any siblings?"

He didn't miss the brief shadow that cast a look of concern on her otherwise angelic features. It was gone as quickly as it had come, however, leaving him wondering if he'd imagined it.

"Not anymore. She died a long time ago, back when I

was a child."

So, no, he hadn't imagined the shadow, even though it was long gone, a smile gracing her face again as if nothing was amiss. Her voice retained a husky quality that would be a turn-on if he didn't know what caused it.

"I'm so sorry, Lissa. I don't mean to pry, but do you mind telling me what happened?"

"I don't. It was so long ago, though, I don't remember many of the details."

"That's fine. I just want to be there for you."

He didn't believe that she didn't recall much—the loss of a sibling wasn't something someone simply got over with time. It stayed, along with the guilt of being left behind to deal with the emotional aftermath. He and Tomás knew a thing or two about that. However, he didn't want to make her more uncomfortable than she already was. Hopefully, they'd have time on their side and could delve into each other's family dynamics more another time.

Though, the thought that such a discussion may be at a family dinner with her and her husband, Tomás, crushed his chest as if a boulder had been placed atop it. He shifted on the chaise, the air suddenly warm.

Maybe he should have gone along with her idea to lighten the mood with another round of exhilarating sex and a nice meal to round off the afternoon. Why had he thought a serious turn of topics was the right move to make when they only had days, at best, weeks together before she wed his brother? He should have spent the remaining time making memories with her naked body to keep him warm at night once she was married off to Tomás. She could share all of the sad stuff about her family with him.

The thing was, he didn't want her to.

He, Gael, was the one who was supposed to hear her heart-wrenching stories. He was the one who should be consoling her when life got too hard to bear. He didn't want to only be a warm body to sate her desires with—he wanted it all, the whole woman and all that came with her, good or otherwise.

"It's pretty simple, actually. Nora was born ten years before me and was subjected to the same bullying my father bestowed upon me. If anything, she had it worse. He never laid a hand on me, most likely because he wanted to avoid the fate he'd created for himself when he abused her, but there was once he hit her so hard he had to call the family physician to care for her. She was in a coma for two days, the only two days my father let up on her."

"Jesus. Why was he so horrible to her?"

She shrugged, her gaze now on the horizon. When she shivered, he took the throw he kept around the back of the chaise and draped it on her shoulders. She didn't budge, still staring distractedly at the shimmering water beneath them, transfixed by a memory or thought Gael wasn't privy to. Finally, she shook her head and gazed back at him, her eyes damp. She'd been through so much. How could he possibly let her father continue to manipulate her into a marriage that would only serve him? The injustice was profound and staggeringly difficult to wade through.

"I guess he saw the life his children had taken from him—he was a wealthy playboy until he knocked my mother up and trapped her in a loveless marriage. She was a princess in Aldonia, so of course he stayed with her for the title it afforded him, but they never loved each other. He resented us, and said so often. But Nora was strong enough to stand up to him and call him on his indiscretions, so she bore the brunt of his anger. I think, as awful as it was, he wanted us gone so he could resume his lifestyle of bedding as many women as he could beneath my mother's nose. He got his way with Nora, and I'm next on the list, I suppose. Though I have no right to complain—at least I'm alive."

"I can't believe my parents haven't seen through the sham. Through *him*. We should tell them." Urgency prickled along his skin.

She smiled up at him, a sad grin that only made him feel worse about her situation.

"I'm sure they know. The royal family in Aldonia—now run by my cousins Robert and Philip, were aware. Bad press can be hidden from the public, but it's impossible to keep from the royal family."

Was that ever the truth. He himself had only escaped ridicule from his country and family by taking up the most sought-after post in the Navy and excelling at it more than any person who'd held the job ever had. His guess was his parents knew about Lissa's father and thought they were doing Lissa a favor by letting her join their family. It was despicable, but not surprising. His father wasn't a gem himself, but he'd never hit him or his brother. Still, he was as interested in social climbing as Lissa's schmuck of a father. A treaty with Aldonia was good for the country, plain and simple.

"So, what happened to her? To Nora?"

He hadn't ever heard of her, nor was any record of her available. He'd spent the last three days doing two things, and two things only: attempting to track down her mystery attacker, and scouring the internet for anything he could find on Lissa's family to see if there was a way out of the marriage bargain she was tied up in. Unfortunately, he'd failed on both accounts, an altogether new feeling for him. If his parents wouldn't relent to an ego-driven abuser, there wasn't much hope they'd give up the fight for something as pitiful to them as love.

"When I was eight, she was promised to a wealthy businessman in China—a deal brokered by my megalomaniac father, as I'm sure you correctly assumed—and she ran away that night. She died in a boating accident on the Black Sea trying to escape. If she hadn't been running from him…" She trailed off and it felt like the air around them cooled twenty degrees. He shivered under the weight of her loss.

She attempted a smile, but he could see the pain behind

her eyes. "Not a very happy story, is it?"

Gael's heart clenched, and his blood ran cold. A surge of hatred so visceral, so profound it scared him, flooded his nervous system. There wasn't a lot of evil he hadn't encountered during his past two years in charge of one of the most elite naval operations in the world, but Lissa's father topped them all.

"It's not, but it explains so much about why you were there, in the Kelles. Why I was able to meet you. You've taken on the burden she used to carry."

"I figured if anyone would understand, it would be you."

His heart warmed at the unintended compliment from her.

"You don't owe them anything, you know that, right? I mean, your sister had the right idea by leaving the moment she was able to do so without looking back. That she had the… accident is just that—an unfortunate tragedy. Perhaps you should consider doing the same—running away that is."

She'd suggested as much, hadn't she? That she'd run away with him?

He understood, though, as soon as he thought it, she'd only proposed running from her arranged marriage, not her family entirely. That was an altogether different, and far more taxing, idea. Still, what did she have to gain by staying tied to them in any way, even as a daughter?

Her eyes turned from emerald to a pine green, dark and hidden behind a shade that had fallen over her face when he'd floated the idea that she leave her family behind. He hadn't meant to sound so harsh, but it was how he felt. Why did she care what those horrible people had to say about her life?

Because they're her parents, idiot.

Yeah, yeah, he wanted to tell his subconscious. He knew all too well the trappings of family and their unrealistic expectations that bound their children with guilt and threats of failure. But that didn't make it any easier watching a woman he cared for deeply go through such an ordeal.

She cleared her throat and trailed a finger along his collarbone.

"So, how about that romp in the sun? I'll bet you're wishing you'd taken me up on it earlier," she said, throwing her shoulders back and tossing him a come-get-me grin. She'd changed the subject rather than answer him, but he saw through her ploy to the reason behind it.

He smiled weakly. As much as forgetting all serious talk and making love to Lissa appealed to him, she was so much more to him than just a hookup. He couldn't let her go back to her parents, nor to his family. If they left the palace, it would mean condemning her to a life devoid of love where she was no more than a pawn in her parents' pull for power. He'd be as bad as her father if he allowed that.

It was as much an impossibility as making love to her while she was engaged to his brother was just hours ago. But the more he learned, the more he loved about her, and the bigger the claim she had on his heart, the harder it was to imagine letting her go.

The truth was, she didn't belong to Tomás any more than she belonged to him. But he could offer her a choice.

"Why don't we run away together? You tried to convince me it was a good idea earlier, but I'm a slow learner. So, what do you say?" he asked. He shot up, clad in nothing more than a beach towel, his partial erection awkwardly holding up the makeshift cover around his waist. "Marry me, Lissa."

The words were out of his mouth before they could work through his carefully set filters that were supposed to stop him from uttering such stupid things aloud. At least before he could think them through. Somehow, her presence bypassed that mechanism in him, and he found himself wondering why marrying her wouldn't be a good idea. Not to mention why he'd wasted three days figuring that out. His brother—if he were remotely aware of what was going on behind his back—would have a thing or two to say about women always getting to the truth faster.

Gael ran through the list building in his head. He could more than care for her financially. And if he married her, it wouldn't give her parents a damn thing, especially since he'd forsaken the crown and all the perks it provided. Everything he had would be hers, but no laws dictated what they would have to share with her conniving parents, especially her sadistic father.

The air became pregnant with anticipation as he awaited her response. It was too much, far too soon, wasn't it? After all, how well did they really know each other? *Mierda*. He'd screwed up...

But then she smiled and hope snuck past his defenses.

"Okay," she said, standing up and joining him, her body naked and gleaming with moisture from their time in the sun. It was tinged a light pink, a sign he needed to whisk her away into the confines of his suite and celebrate with her where she wasn't at risk of being sunburnt. She laughed again, this time a joyous sound that wormed its way into his heart.

As quickly as it did, however, a sense of dread clouded the happiness, casting a shadow over the moment. It took a moment for his mind to register the switch and discern the reason behind it.

If they did this, *really* did this, he'd be cast out of his family forever. He'd be a traitor to his country, and all the explanations in the world wouldn't help clear his name. And what would become of Tomás if Gael stole his bride-to-be? Sure, this situation helped her, but he'd vowed to look after his brother after they lost Michelle, their sister. This wasn't doing a good job of that.

These were the thoughts he would have had before he sprang the question on her if only his internal filter was at all functional.

Now, it was too late. He'd asked, and she'd accepted.

He tried to tell himself it didn't matter, that all he needed was her, that Tomás would recover, but as she wrapped her arms around him tightly, her breath warm on his skin that already felt too hot, too uncomfortable, his breath hitched in his throat.

Good God. What the hell had he done?

CHAPTER SIX

It would all be okay. Right?

Right?

No matter how many times she asked herself, she wasn't convinced. Sure, she was being handed everything she'd wanted her whole life—financial and emotional freedom from her parents while tying herself to the man who'd claimed her heart and branded her body two years ago—but like this?

She paced the floor of her suite, her feet unable to still the rest of her body, or vice versa. It was as if a live wire ran from her brain, direct through her heart, spreading out to her limbs from there. Gael's proposal had sent a surge of energy through that wire that threatened to short circuit her faculties.

At least fourteen dresses, four mismatched silk tops and slacks, and a dozen pairs of shoes lay strewn on the floor. Gael had told her to wear something casual, something warm, with the only caveat that they were going out somewhere safe to celebrate. Though, she hadn't a clue what she owned that matched his vague request. She was well aware her wardrobe was enviable in many circles, however, it seemed ill-fitting for going anywhere with her future husband.

At least he wasn't there to see the disarray his query had caused. She must look like a feral animal on the prowl, her curls frizzy and face splotchy with the exertion of overthinking yet another problem. He'd left her alone in order to "get started on the process" for the wedding, but every second he was away, locked in his office again, no doubt, she second-guessed her acquiescence.

She held up a black silk tunic and a matching pair of slacks but threw them down with disgust on top of the growing pile of discarded frocks. Ugh. Why couldn't she just let a good thing happen to her without picking it apart and ruining it?

Because the bottom always drops out in the end, doesn't it?

As much as she wanted to tell her subconscious—the nosy jerk—to shove it, she had to admit her innermost critic had a point. What she needed to do was figure out specifically why this new development bothered her so much. After all, hadn't she more or less asked him for the same thing when she'd told him she'd run away with him? Why was she concerned now that he'd actually agreed?

Because you don't do relationships. You wouldn't even know where to start.

Not true, she admonished her subconscious. Well, not entirely. She didn't know how to do relationships, sure, but that wasn't the issue.

As soon as the flutters in her heart that took off like wild pheasants in her chest when he'd asked her calmed, the reality of the situation set in. She wanted this, all of it, all of him, but she wanted to come by it honestly. This fly-by-the-seat-of-his-pants proposal was romantic in theory, but the more she thought about it, it wasn't really different from the marriage she was being forced into before Gael came into her life. It was still a way to manage her parents' expectations of her and get her free of them.

Yes, she liked—no, loved—Gael, but this wasn't the way it was supposed to happen for them.

Where was the romance, the courting, and fairy-tale proposal? What about her dream wedding and happily-ever-after? How could they build a life together, allowing Gael to pursue his military career when she didn't even know who she was outside of her parents' savior? What would she want to do with her life, her career? If they started a family, what kind of role models would they be when the only reason they were together was to protect her from her family? Could she and Gael be truly happy when their marriage began under duress and secrecy?

More than any of those pressing questions about how his proposal affected her, she couldn't imagine what this quick proposal and shotgun wedding would do to Gael's relationship with his parents and brother.

Would Gael resent her for the quick wedding sans his family? Besides, what about the other ramifications? What would derailing the royal wedding plans do to his chances in the military? Worse yet, what were the consequences facing his brother and his marital situation if she and Gael eloped?

So many questions plagued her, and the most frustrating thing about all of them was that not only didn't she have anything resembling an answer, but she couldn't talk through the concerns with Gael. Not without making him think she didn't care about him as much as she did.

After all, he'd asked and she said yes.

It was so simple, yet at the same time more convoluted than winding around the Aldonian one-way streets after dark. Accepting his proposal had seemed like a good idea in the split second she'd had to consider a way out of the mess with her folks. But now, it appeared to be a death sentence for him, no matter how much it aided her situation.

She had to talk to him, help him understand that she loved him and wanted to be with him forever, but a rash proposal and wedding weren't the answer for either of them to get what they wanted long term. And she had to do it now, before she lost her nerve.

She was halfway out her door to find him before he got too far down the impromptu wedding to-do list, when she ran head first into a wall of muscled flesh. Warm, inviting, muscled male flesh. Her stomach flipped with desire.

"Oh!" she gasped in surprise. Shock quickly turned into a wave of lust as she took in the man before her. Just when she thought Gael couldn't get any more handsome or alluring, he had to show up in a white organza button-down t-shirt and tan slacks, both of which showed off an enviable winter tan and sinewy, bulky forearms she knew firsthand were capable of lifting her by her hips and pressing her against the wall.

She shook her head out of the sex-laced fog he created whenever he was around.

Suddenly, why she'd been so quick to say yes to his strange proposal hit her with blunt force. When Gael Reyes was within six feet of her, her ability to form a coherent thought flew right out the satin drapes. Even then, a fully formed plan hatched about how to get what they both wanted without having to run away together in the middle of the night at the ready, she couldn't recall a word of why she'd thought marrying him today wasn't the best idea she'd ever had.

Damn men and their sexiness that overrode critical thought.

"Well, hello there, future bride. I see you haven't decided on an outfit for tonight," he mused, a crooked half smile turning his handsome features into beacons of mischief. She flat-out forgot why she was on her way to finding him before she ran into him. Literally. He always did have a way of making her feel optimistic about stuff she overly worried about. She let out a breath she didn't know she was holding in.

"You told me to dress warm. While we're on the tropical beaches of Spain. And you're in an outfit that would have worked in the Kelles. Not much help, are you?"

He grinned, and the heat building in her stomach roared, sending the blaze coursing through her veins. Maybe she wouldn't need anything to keep her warm if he kept looking at her like that. As if he'd read her thoughts, a wicked grin spread further across his face.

"We can always go naked and keep each other warm. I've got a few ideas about how to make that work…" He trailed off when she landed a playful slug on his shoulder.

"Ha ha. No, it's just that even though I brought half my wardrobe, nothing fits your description. It would help if I knew where we were going."

"Not a chance, Princess." He winked. "Surprises are half the fun. Just wear something casual, and uh, bring a jacket. It'll just be us."

"Just us, huh?" Her voice wavered, belying her now-constant fear about being outside the confines of the beach house and its trusted guard. She was excited at the idea of a real date with Gael, but the reality of why they were there, on the southern point of the Cantabrian Sea instead of planning a wedding at the Galician palace, settled heavily on her shoulders. There was a threat on her life, and they still didn't have a clue who was behind it.

It was too easy to get wrapped up in Gael's crystalline-blue eyes and forget there was anything less innocuous than a week with him by her side for her to contend with.

"Don't you worry, little lady. I won't let anything happen to you. When I said 'just us', I meant us and a throng of guards a safe but invisible distance away. I need you safe, Lissa, but I have no intention of them seeing what I do to you." He tucked his head in the crook of her neck and nibbled on the lobe of her ear. Any thought of criminals who may or may not be bent on her destruction evaporated from her mind, replaced with thoughts of how to get the man now sucking on the same earlobe naked again.

Still, she was touched he understood her reticence to

leave the cozy home they'd created for themselves and venture out into the world. And as usual, without her having to say a word.

On their second morning together in the Kelles, Gael had shown up with a double espresso and warmed almond milk for her when she'd gotten out of the shower. The morning before, he'd observed her ordering the same from room service and had not only recalled her order verbatim, but was kind enough to bring her a to-go cup of her ritualistic morning brew the next day. That was only one of a dozen small moments where he seemed to read her mind, discern her desires long before she was even aware of them.

"Thank you, Gael. You always seem to know what I need. I'm not that worried about the threat, not with you by my side."

It was true, too. Gael didn't just give her a sense of security when it came to her physical well-being, but her emotional welfare as well. She'd been seen for who she truly was for the first time by him in the islands. Since then, he was the only person to have ever cared for her without agenda. She wasn't used to someone offering her something without demanding a pound of flesh in return.

It was disorienting, the weightlessness of unconditional affection. Tempting, too.

She turned her head and intersected the delicate kisses he peppered along her neck with her mouth. She ran her tongue along the place where their mouths met and felt the groan he let loose vibrate and tickle her lips.

He was close enough that his pleasure rose hard and strong against her thigh. That she had this kind of effect on him was an empowering and altogether heady feeling. Dampness flooded the bare space between her thighs, fortunately hidden behind the towel she wore after her shower.

"Hurry and pick something to wear so I can whisk you away and remove your clothing as soon as possible. After we celebrate an early Christmas, that is." He pulled back, and with no more than a knowing wink, left her alone in her room. An ache in her stomach sent a wave of heat and more moisture to her center. Good God, would she ever tire of wanting this man? She didn't think it was possible.

But her heart hitched at the idea of an early holiday. She hoped that meant lying naked in front of a fire and not gifts or carols or anything of that nature. Why hadn't she thought of the fact that Christmas was sneaking up on them? She didn't have anything to give him, but then how would she have procured a gift when she was hidden away in some unknown royal family property in the furthest northwest corner of her new country? And not especially when she usually went about her days avoiding Christmas and its trappings of false happiness and family togetherness.

Unease swept over her like a tidal wave, catching her off guard.

On top of the marriage, either to Gael or his brother, the looming threat on her life that compounded exponentially the moment they left the relative safety of their hideout, and her parents and their conniving ways to get what they wanted at her expense, now she had to find a way to celebrate a holiday that had never brought her any happiness? With a man she loved but who wasn't aware of any of the reasons why this idea filled her with dread?

So, tell him.

Ha! As if it were that easy… Her subconscious was out of control and completely wrong about this little detail of her life.

How could she fill him in on those particularly distressing memories when she'd already sidelined the afternoon with a woeful tale about her sister and father, one that she'd rather have forgotten than share with a man she didn't want to scare away? Maybe at some point, but not now, not at the start of their… whatever they were doing.

At least she had Gael at her side as she conquered the holiday. And she would enjoy that—or enjoy *him*—no matter how much distress it caused her.

Ugh. There seemed no way to get out of it, save canceling the proposal Gael had made earlier that day. Which, of course, would lead to a multitude of other, far worse scenarios. No, she had to go through with this. It was far too late for anything else.

An hour later, Lissa found herself clad in a loose-fitting sweater with a luxurious cowl neck, fleece-lined tights, and snow boots in the second most surprising place she'd ever expected to be—in a helicopter headed straight for the snow-covered Pyrenees in the middle of what looked like a building storm behind them. The only place she'd be more surprised to be heading was home, to her parents. Had she known she'd be hovering two-thousand feet above the earth in a flying iron death trap, she might have wished for the latter.

She grasped Gael's arm as tight as she could, but it didn't assuage the growing sense of dread that swirled inside her stomach like smoke. She'd never flown in a helicopter, and for good reason. Wasn't it every week that one of these crashed into the Aldonian foothills—far less formidable peaks than they headed to at that moment— and killed everyone aboard? Her teeth chattered despite the heat in the cabin, and her jaw was sore from clenching it so tightly.

Even though this one was like something out of a movie, with its leather interior highlighted by wood floors, gold-lined inlaid drink holders that currently held her untouched crystal flute of champagne, and a flatscreen television playing an old rom-com she'd watched countless times, it didn't do anything to settle her queasy stomach.

"Are you okay?" Gael asked.

Am I? A quick check of her pulse would tell her she was about to suffer a panic attack, but that would only make things worse. She concentrated on taking slow breaths in and out. She looked over at him, trying not to notice the lightning off in the distance, closing in quick on them. An attempt at a smile failed when the Eurocopter dropped a couple of feet without warning. A cry of fear escaped her lips, and she stared up at Gael, hoping he would calm her.

Instead, the peaceful smile he wore only served to add frustration to her already frayed nerves. How was he so damned serene when the world was falling down around them?

"We're okay, Liss. It's just some basic turbulence. Come here," he said, drawing himself over to her seat. In a swift movement that barely seemed to jostle her at all, he placed her on his lap, her head cradled in the nook of his shoulder. He pressed a button she couldn't see, and the leather armchair reclined until it was as flat as her mattress at home, only twice as comfortable.

Okay, maybe this wasn't so bad after all. If she had to leave this world, at least she'd do so in royal comfort.

"So, I figured I should tell you where we're going now that we're almost there." While she was well aware he was only sharing his previously guarded secret locale to distract her, she didn't care. It was working.

"Yes, please. I'd love to know why you whisked me away from the warmth and sunshine to send us careening in an airborne death cage toward ice and certain doom."

He laughed, a booming, all-encompassing chortle she'd only heard once or twice since they met. It did the trick, loosening the chains that seemed bent on pulling her down in a spiral of negative thinking. In fact, it got rid of them altogether.

"Well, *cariña*, as much as I loved watching you prance around in that gold bikini, I wanted to take you somewhere special, somewhere that means everything to me because it's the first thing I earned on my own. Built on my own. Which, of course, means it isn't marred by memories of my tumultuous past. You'll do me the honor of being my first guest."

Lissa's body temperature shot up a degree or two hearing that.

"It's like your fortress of solitude," she said, laughing. Despite her fear that she and Gael would chop a yet unforeseen eagle with their rotor blades and plummet to their deaths, she hadn't been this relaxed in months, years even. Almost two years to the day, as fate would have it.

What was it about this man that he could rile her up so that every nerve stood on end, only to calm her so quickly and completely she could forget a crazy person was out to kill her and she was being forced to marry a complete stranger?

He was magic, pure and simple. Handsome as sin, built like a Greek god, *magic*. And hers if she could just get past the logical side of her brain telling her marrying him wasn't a good idea.

"Fortress of what?" he asked, confusion lacing his words.

"Solitude. Like in Superman. It's his secret place where he learns who he is, and the only person he ever brings there is Lois Lane, his true love. Not that I'm saying I'm your true love or anything. It's just an analogy from a movie I used to watch with Nora…" she trailed off, feeling like a prized idiot.

Way to go, Lissa. Scare him off with all that soulmate crap.

The thing was, she didn't have a clue how to have a normal relationship outside her role as Princess of Aldonia. She was never allowed to date, and though she had a healthy appreciation for the opposite sex, that didn't mean she had a clue how to *talk* to one she was interested in. Sex, she could do. But feelings and emotions and all that mushy stuff? It wasn't as if she had the best role models for that. Which was part of why the impending holiday had her riled up.

"Then yes," he said, tipping her chin up so that their mouths met in the middle. "It is my fortress of solitude.

As long as you'll be my Lois."

Then he went and said something sweet and perfectly timed, per usual. It made her feel simultaneously like kissing and kicking him, the former for being the most caring man she'd ever met, and the latter for highlighting what a screw-up she was for not thinking of sweet things to say in response.

She really did need to practice this whole art-of-seduction-outside-the-bedroom thing.

And just like that, the Super Puma landed with what could only be described as a purr despite the gale-force winds and weather—that now included snow and sleet, to her horror.

She exhaled a sigh of relief, to which Gael could only laugh. She saw how she might have exaggerated the certain death she was sure they were headed for, but up there, the only thing that could get her to see past it was Gael and his strength, his humor.

If that wasn't a microcosm of how her worldview was shaped of late, what was?

Gael whisked her up a steep driveway that had a thin layer of frozen ball bearings in the form of hail covering it. More than once she was only held upright by the wind coming up behind her and Gael's steady arm at her back. When they finally reached the end of the walk, she was too wind-blasted to see what she'd walked into, and it took her a few seconds of shaking the ice from her hair and brushing it off her shoulders to look up once she got inside.

Any breath she had left from the strenuous walk up the drive was slammed out of her in a gasp that echoed off the cavernous walls. Gael had drastically undersold his fortress of solitude. Where Superman's was cold and clean, monochromatic and harsh lines, Gael's mountain retreat was nothing short of its opposite in all the best ways.

It was warm and bright despite the darkness creeping in on it from the outside world, and it instantly felt like home.

She gaped up at the bird's eye maple beams bracing the cathedral ceilings and smiled. Her cousin, King Robert of Aldonia, just had a countryside home built for his new wife and used the same rare wood. Great men with great tastes.

The stone flooring should have been cool and uninviting, but the warm red and orange undertones made it an oasis in the frozen desert beyond their doors. Tastefully decorated with American Southwest art, the home—or retreat, or whatever he called it—was a gem unlike any she'd happened across on all her travels.

To top it all off, it was given just enough Christmas spirit to warm her soul to the idea without vomiting yuletide all over the place and turning her off. Again, it was as if he anticipated her needs without her ever having to utter a word.

Was there anything sexier?

A quick glance at the man in his tan slacks, industrial suede boots, and a leather bomber jacket, dark features accentuated by even darker lust argued there just might be. Her insides liquified under his stare.

"Gael. It's… it's…" she just couldn't find the words to express how lovely she found the space, and how deeply she regretted whining about leaving the beach. Of course he'd known she'd love it here, and of course she should just get in the habit of trusting him. When had he ever let her down?

The unique proposal from earlier that day—was it really only just hours ago he'd asked her to marry him?— came to mind, but that didn't even seem so crazy now, standing here with Gael. In fact, it seemed the logical, romantic thing to do, as if they'd been dating the whole two years since they met. He hadn't brought it up since he'd originally proposed the idea, though, so the ball was in his court about when the proceedings should take place. Maybe he'd relax enough here to let her in, to talk to her about his ideas for them.

"It isn't the beach, I'll give you that." He chuckled, peering around her shoulder to the now raging storm that beat against the tempered glass and stone. "But will it do for the week? I wanted it to feel like the holidays, and this place seemed perfect."

"I don't have the words to tell you just how lovely it is." And she didn't. He perpetually left her breathless, thoughtless, and wordless, none of which she was used to experiencing. "Why didn't your father suggest it as our original hideout?" she asked. Following his gaze to the windows, there didn't seem to be any question that attacking them there, in a veritable castle with one entrance and fortified by the most rugged peaks she'd ever seen, would be a feat not even the most professional hitmen would attempt.

"My father doesn't know this place exists. Like I said, it's my personal space, and you're its first guest. I couldn't imagine sharing it with anyone else, Lissa."

Heat rose in her cheeks, showing off how much that simple compliment meant to her. "Well, I don't think I've ever shared Christmas with a lovelier space, or company. Thank you."

"You're welcome." He cleared his throat and broke her gaze, gesturing to the simple decorations adorning an eighteen-foot tree, some candles and holly intimate and discreet on the hearth. "I, um, took a guess that family-centric events like Christmas weren't going to be high on your list of pleasant memories, but maybe we could start to make some of our own?"

She felt like he'd punched her in the chest, his words slammed into her so heavy and quick. He'd posed the idea like a request, but she couldn't imagine anything more perfect. There was no question in her mind he was everything she'd ever want, could ever need.

"How do you do that?" she asked.

"Do what?" He closed the distance between them and

rubbed her shoulders affectionately. Tears came unbidden to her eyes, burning them with shame. She'd never had anyone, *anyone*, see her as clearly as Gael did, and he did it so effortlessly and with so much love attached. He'd even made her feel that way the night she'd met him.

Seen. Admired. Appreciated.

It felt so welcome it scared her to her core. History seemed bent on proving to her that this kind of serenity didn't last, at least not for her, but she'd damn well appreciate it while she had it.

When his lips brushed the furrowed skin of her forehead, heat circled around her and snaked its way inside her chest.

"You have a way of knowing just what I need before I even know it myself."

"Should I take that as a compliment?" He smiled but seemed unsure of himself.

She nodded vigorously. "You should. Your intuition is eerily on point, but I'm not complaining. And the holiday touch is just right. You weren't wrong in thinking it hasn't always been a happy holiday for me, but I'm excited to start over with you."

She meant it, too. The idea of making a life, a home with the man currently nibbling on her earlobe and sending waves of desire rushing through her was so tempting, so thrilling that it overrode all her fears.

"I'm glad." He pulled back, a concerned look on his face that didn't echo his words. "Do you want to talk about that? Your unhappy holidays, I mean? I'm here for anything you have to tell me. Nothing is off limits, *cariña.*"

Lissa warmed at the endearment but shook her head. "No. Thank you, and maybe someday we can open that particular compartment of Pandora's box, but right now I want our lips to get to work in a way that doesn't involve forming words."

A twinge of guilt settled in the back of her mind at the smile Gael shot her. Sure, it was her intention to thwart any uncomfortable discussion with the mind-blowing sex she knew would help get her mind off her problems, but that didn't make it sit any easier. Gael was kind, giving, and the most intelligent man she'd ever met. Using him for sex was beneath them both, and he certainly deserved more.

The problem was that she didn't have much more to offer at the moment. She wanted to bare herself to him—emotionally as well as physically—but what good did that do him? Who knew if they'd get away with their plans to marry, or if that would lead to them sharing a life together? Especially when two sets of parents seemed bent on her marrying the other Reyes brother.

Why not let them both enjoy the time they had together doing what brought them both a pretty decent amount of joy? To that end, she placed her hands on the back pockets of his slacks and squeezed, giggling when he let out a growl against her neck.

Yes, that was how she wanted to spend her time.

He raked his teeth along the sensitive skin of her neck, and a purr of delight tickled her throat. This man...

A jarring and altogether unwelcome chime from Gael's phone echoed off the walls in the cathedral-like space. *No!* Her heart screamed. She desperately wanted to keep heading where they were heading, and that was off the table with the intrusion of the outside world. Gael had informed her when they first left for the Cantabrian house the phone he brought was only in case of emergencies; only Tomás had the number, which meant their evening was decidedly on hold for the time being.

Why, was another question altogether, one that sent stones of dread sinking into her lower abdomen. It wasn't good news that infiltrated their previous peace, that was for sure.

Gael pulled away, a frown carved into his perfectly tanned and kissable features.

An ache rose in her chest, burning like a small ball of fire in her throat. Half of it stemmed from her unquenched desire for Gael, the other half from dread of what the call would mean for them. She didn't want to go home, not when she was just starting to loosen up and enjoy herself. Not to mention the fact that if they were called back now, there was no safety net to catch them. She would be forced to marry Tomás.

Gael met her gaze, her own concern and lust reflected in his eyes.

"I have to get this. Hold that thought?" he asked. His voice was serious, but he tried to play off a smile that only served to highlight his own growing worry.

"Of course."

He flipped open the phone and then walked out of the entryway and into a room she couldn't see from where she stood. All she caught was a screaming voice on the other end, berating them for leaving the safety of the beach house without permission. If they only knew the stronghold he'd delivered her to, they wouldn't be so angry. Poor Gael. He was at the same mercy of his parents as she was hers, it seemed. Perhaps now, he'd see how futile it was to try and fight that.

When the door slammed, cutting off his muffled discussion, she fought the urge to follow him. Was he really going to have a conversation that was likely about her, about her safety, behind a closed door? Again?

She bristled, her gut warning her off storming in there and demanding he speak in front of her like an equal. The harsh reality was that she wasn't an equal. She was no more than a pawn passed between her parents and their play for power and a man she didn't know or want to be with. Then, meanwhile, the man she loved was keeping her in the dark about issues that affected her.

With sudden clarity, she remembered why she didn't date. Okay, fine. Her parents forbid her from having a serious relationship with a guy who wasn't on their shortlist for potential husbands-who-would-fund-the-family, but being a princess meant men treated her like the cartoon version of one. Which was precisely why she spent a majority of her time seeking anonymity in hookups rather than investing emotionally. It was so much easier that way—all the fun with none of the drama or hurt feelings.

Turned out she wasn't missing much on the emotional front, was she? Gael was just another man treating her like a damsel in distress he needed to save, which couldn't be further from the truth.

Ugh. Men.

When Gael didn't reappear for several minutes, she left her bags where they lay and set off to explore. Screw waiting for the official tour—she could take care of herself, and even though it was a small gesture of independent defiance on her part, it felt good not to bide her time waiting on Gael. Aside from the mind-altering sex, it seemed since he'd reappeared in her life, that was all she'd been doing.

Well, not anymore.

She began at the room to her right, which as luck would have it was a full bar, complete with mahogany walls and stained-glass mosaics of what must have been the mountain range they were nestled in. She swallowed back a gasp of wanton appreciation as she examined the one-of-a-kind bartop, a single slab of cedar sanded down enough to show her reflection in its gloss, but with its original siding. The uneven edges gave the bar a polished yet rustic look that was hard to replicate. A quick assessment of the thing put it at around thirty feet long. God, it must have been a Herculean feat to get the slab up the mountain. She hoped he'd attempted the flight in better weather than they arrived in.

She gave the woodworking the time and appreciation it deserved and then found what she was hoping she'd come across. A floor-to-mile-high-ceiling wine room attached to the rest of the bar with a stunning stained-glass mosaic of a vineyard acting as the door. In keeping with her "I can take care of myself" mantra, she let herself in and perused until she found a Rothschild red blend she wouldn't get herself in too much trouble for opening but that might just make Gael regret leaving her to fend for herself. In less than a minute, she'd located a corkscrew, and thirty seconds later, she was on her way out of the bar in search of a new room to explore, a healthy pour of the wine in hand.

Any impression of the place she'd made when she first stepped through the door was nothing compared to the awe the rest of the rooms inspired. From the bar, she made her way from one overly impressive room to the next. Gael hadn't left a single desire left unmet.

From the en suite hot tub in the master bedroom to the library with the same bird's eye maple from the entrance used for built-ins, every inch of the humble mountain mansion left her reeling with pride. He may be a prince by blood, a naval captain by trade, but he was a craftsman at heart, that much was obvious.

In the last room, a small, almost hidden office off the master suite, she came across an ornate yet simplistic desk that looked like it was made of ebony and elm. They were two of the rarest woods on the market—a little-known fact her money-grubbing father had shared with her when she demanded he explain why a forty-thousand Euro bookshelf arrived at their home the previous summer. He didn't even read.

"Because it's the best," he'd told her, and why that answer hadn't occurred to her first was boggling. Of course her father would want the top-of-the-line, most expensive version of an object he'd never use to flaunt his perceived wealth and importance. Only she knew different. He was as broke as an American used-car salesman and just as smarmy.

The recherché desk in what appeared to be Gael's study was another thing altogether. It suited the room, the aesthetic of the home, and the man who owned it.

What might appear to be a parade of ostentatiousness in her father's home looked rugged and earned in Gael's. She settled into the plush leather chair behind the desk and sipped at her wine. Why hadn't Gael brought anyone else here? It was so charming, so perfectly *him*, she couldn't understand the secret.

When she set her glass on a cork-lined coaster at the back of the desk, her eye caught a copper-framed photo of a small child that couldn't have been more than a year and a half old. Lissa did a double-take and brought the photo closer. Her stomach flipped when she recognized the ink-black curls and crystalline-blue eyes staring back at her as the same as those that had just left her to take a call. The resemblance was uncanny, but it would require some pretty heavy explaining.

Because though the picture looked like Gael as a child, it so very clearly wasn't.

Unless Gael wore diamond-stud earrings and pink lacy frocks as a child, that was. Lissa's stomach settled from the initial surprise only to plummet to her knees. Why was a picture of a little girl hidden away in the corner-most location in a house that was as much a secret as the photo? Nothing similar existed at the beach house, which she would know since in his three-day sojourn into his private office, she'd treated herself to a similar ceiling-to-floor tour. This was hidden for a reason, but once again, only an unanswered *why* made itself available by means of an explanation.

After a few moments of staring at the photo, only one response presented itself. But that couldn't be it, *could it?*

Did Gael have a *child?*

God, she hoped not. It would complicate everything so much more. More than she had the willingness to put up with, at least according to her initial reaction which included bile rising to meet the dread in the back of her throat.

It would make sense why he'd been so reticent to hook

back up with Lissa a couple of weeks ago. It would also put the girl at almost exactly a year old if she was born a year or so after Lissa met Gael in the Kelles. Plenty of time to meet another woman and have her child.

Okay, okay, she needed to calm the hell down. This could be anyone. His niece, for instance. *He's only got one brother whom you are supposed to marry. Try again.*

Ugh. She needed to find a way to suffocate that overly nosy subconscious of hers before she overthought yet another aspect of being with Gael. They were beginning to pile up.

But this time, the racing thoughts—the same ones competing with her heart that desperately wanted to believe in Gael—were right. He didn't have any other siblings other than Tomás, and the likelihood her betrothed was able to pull off a secret love child as the future king was less believable than the obvious truth.

Gael was a father.

A chill raced over her skin at the same time her chest felt like it was being engulfed in flames. So, this was why he'd brought her there. To tell her. If they got married, he couldn't keep a child a secret from her. But what of the mother? Was she still in the picture? Was this the *real* reason he'd been relegated to the military—not at his request as he'd made Lissa believe, but because of a scandal involving an illegitimate birth?

She stared hard at the child's photo, a sense of doom spreading through her veins like poison. Only one question of the myriad that plagued her broke through the noise, louder than the rest, demanding to be heard.

Could she handle being a mother if he asked her to?

Or rather, could she take what she'd learned about what *not* to do—the only type of role models her parents had been—and turn that into a loving relationship? She didn't know the first thing about being responsible for another human being. In fact, she'd operated under the exact opposite premise most of her life. She wasn't a damsel in distress, nor was she someone who took care of others.

She was alone, with only herself to worry about, protect, and care for.

For the most part, she was okay with that arrangement, but at that precise moment, it felt like she was woefully unprepared for almost everything being thrown at her— being a wife, a potential mother-figure—what could she possibly offer anyone else?

For crying out loud, she couldn't even stomach the thought of Christmas without breaking into a cold sweat. How on earth was she supposed to give a little girl the holidays of her dreams when she hadn't healed from the nightmare that was her own childhood?

Her breath caught in her lungs, thick and almost liquid with heat. Her chest constricted, tightening around her ribcage as if it meant to crush her. Her skin turned cold and clammy despite the liquid fire raging through her veins. Jesus. Was this a panic attack? She'd never actually experienced one herself, but her mother was prone to them when her father acted up.

She bent over and put her head between her legs, as she'd seen her mother do hundreds of times, hoping it would help. When it didn't, she seriously considered screaming for help. Not that he'd hear her behind the solid oak door to whatever mystery room he'd disappeared behind.

Luckily—or unluckily—before she could make a decision, she heard her name being called from a distance. Despite her anxiety over his secret and what to do about it, Gael's voice, like the rest of his presence, did the trick, and her breathing and body temperature regulated.

Thank God.

"*Cariña*, are you here?"

She nodded silently, aware that it wouldn't do anything to help him discern her whereabouts, but also unable to do anything about it. Her voice hadn't recovered as quickly as her breath.

Instead, she steeled herself against the onslaught of emotions and feelings that crashed against her now that the initial attack had subsided. Just as quickly, she stood up, straightened her sweater, and calmed her hair back into place.

Not now. She couldn't collapse yet. She needed time to think, time at least until he got the nerve to tell her himself why she was there, and what he had to share with her. She exhaled the remainder of the breath that had gotten stuck in her lungs. Maybe it was a good thing she'd gone exploring and found out the truth for herself.

She'd bought herself time with the idea before it became real.

The only question was, what would she do with that insider knowledge when he made it real?

CHAPTER SEVEN

"There you are," he said, his heart slowing to its normal rhythm as soon as her fiery red hair came into view. Then, like it hadn't slowed at all, his pulse went into overdrive as he took in the tall, statuesque form of the woman he loved compactly settled into the overstuffed armchair in the corner of his office opposite his desk. Every damned time he saw her, his body acted like it was seeing her for the first time again. Would he ever get used to her in his world, sharing his space, living beside him? God, he hoped not.

She held up a glass of wine in a silent response to his greeting and took a long swallow. It was sexy as sin watching the liquid pour down her throat, spotting the drop of burgundy liquid on her lip that her tongue greedily slaked over, making his pants grow tight around the zipper again. Another side effect that seemed to occur every time he laid eyes on her.

"And I see you found the wine fridge. I hope you opened something good. I was planning on toasting us when I got off the phone."

"Oh, yes? What are we toasting, exactly?"

He bristled at the reply, shriller than the typically

confident but tender tone of voice she used with him. Was it just his sensitivity when it came to her and reading between the lines, or was she pissed?

"Um, yeah. I'd like to toast bringing you here, to talking about our future and all the joys and challenges that may lie ahead. I made some headway with our wedding preparations and they should be underway after we can put this mess behind us. There's a lot to celebrate, don't you think? But first I'd like to talk to you about what Tomás called about. Is that okay?"

She didn't respond right away, just peered at him through eyes that seemed to cut right through to the core of him. Was she mad because he left her to take the call? He got why that might have rubbed her the wrong way, but he'd done it very much on purpose. He couldn't talk to his brother around her, not if keeping Lissa safe was the mission, which right now, it was. He could barely concentrate when she was around, not on anything other than stripping her bare right where she stood and burying his head between her legs. That wouldn't go over well with her still-betrothed, his brother.

As for the alarming contents of the call, he'd share those just after he had a chance to relax alongside Lissa. Liquor in some form or another would be a requisite to hashing out the tip Tomás had called to confirm. Then, maybe with both behind them, they could relax and enjoy their holiday together. He had more than a couple of surprises up his sleeve and couldn't wait to share them with Liss. He'd only been telling a half-truth when it came to their wedding preparations. He had every intention of marrying her there, in the home he'd built for them. He just needed the storm to pass so he could fly up his Chaplain from the Navy.

Finally, she cleared her throat and pasted a smile on her face. "There *is* a lot to celebrate. Here, let's get you a glass of wine and you can fill me in."

Gael exhaled a sigh of relief. If she was mad about

anything before, that storm at least seemed to have passed. And a good thing, too. He'd built up this particular moment with her for the past two years in his mind. All he'd dreamt when he built this place was what she'd think of it, especially since he'd taken so much of what she told him she loved about the homes she grew up in and poured it into the design. It was an escape constructed for them, but before that, for him to appreciate the brief time he had with her in the islands, a sort of commemoration of their fleeting but intimate affair. So, it went without saying he was looking forward to that evening with her in the space he'd created for them.

More than physically, too, though his pants were uncomfortably tight where his ardent appreciation of her envisioned bringing her up to his feather pillow-topped bed and devouring her from top to her perfectly manicured, ruby-red toes. With special interest paid right along her center.

No, he wanted that something fierce, but he also couldn't wait to just talk to her. With the strange circumstances surrounding their reunion, followed by the threat on her life, then his inability to free himself of the guilt of still loving her when she was engaged to someone else— no matter if that was her decision or not—he hadn't had a chance just to catch up with her since they'd first relaid eyes on each other. He wanted to hear every last detail—good, bad, and otherwise—of where she'd been, what she'd been up to.

The woman was a drug to him, and he intended to overdose on her as often as possible.

They walked back down to the kitchen, but Lissa stayed an arm's length from his touch, no matter how clipped his pace. He longed to hold her hand, to touch her skin, but she seemed bent on avoiding him. Maybe whatever pissed her off earlier hadn't settled as much as she was letting on.

If there was any doubt her chilly demeanor was aimed at him, it was solidified when they arrived at his kitchen.

She stared him down with icy appraisal the whole time she navigated the space as if she'd been there a week, not an hour. She grabbed a stemless crystal goblet, filled it more than three-quarters full, and gruffly handed it to him. Wine sloshed over the rim of the glass, landing on his hand and the countertop like blood splatters at a crime scene.

Yeah, something was definitely up.

"Are you okay, Liss?" he asked. Of course, she wasn't, but he needed to hear it from her so he could fix whatever the hell he'd done wrong and they could get on with their night. He'd imagined a lot of ways the evening could go, but none of them involved being in a freeze-off with the woman he loved.

"I'm fine. Why wouldn't I be?" Her words felt like frozen daggers piercing his too-warm skin. While he should have felt a chill wafting off her icy stare, instead, it was like he stood in the center of a fire pit. He took off the jacket he'd forgotten he was wearing, but the heat didn't dissipate.

Holy Hell. The steward had certainly done his job stoking the fireplaces before their arrival as instructed. He unbuttoned the top two buttons on his shirt, and it still felt like he was on fire. Probably because of the woman staring at him like he guarded the gates of Hell himself. What could possibly have changed in such a short period of time?

"Because you're acting like I'm a stranger outside an abandoned factory asking if you want free candy right now. Half an hour ago, we were making out in the entryway like a couple of horny teenagers. Forgive me if I find the change a little jarring and unexpected."

Okay, he should really step outside and let the storm cool him down before he popped a blood vessel. It wasn't like him to be so hot under the collar. Literally and figuratively. It was just that this woman got to him. In all the best, and worst, ways.

"Oh, well, I'm sorry my libido didn't last the hour alone

in a house I've never seen, in a place I've never been, in a storm I'd never survive if I left. God forbid you sit me down and treat me like an equal, Gael. You know, marrying you or your brother is really just a toss of the coin. Either way, it looks like I'll be getting a husband who thinks I'm not much more than arm candy. Don't need much trust for that, I'd assume. Not that you've given me much, either way."

Her chest shook with the exertion the rant, her cheeks flushed a vibrant pink. She looked wild, uncontained, and even though she was clearly peeved at him, he'd never been more turned on. What a chump he was. Leaving her alone for so long then blaming her for an attitude? Getting her riled up only to have her respond in kind? Then finding her annoyance arousing?

It was beneath him. All of it. Hell, it was even beneath a man-whore like Tomás used to be.

He sighed and raked his fingers through his hair, not giving a damn about anything except fixing this. All he'd wanted to do was keep her safe and he'd ended up alienating her like her parents did, like any other royal schmuck would have. This was so not okay, and he needed to make it right. Like, *now*.

"I'm sorry," he said. He meant it, too. Almost as much as the three words he felt bubbling up inside his chest, desperate to get out. He swallowed them back, fear shoving them down into the pit of his stomach for now. It wasn't the time. He didn't want to scare her off with an apology and declaration of eternal devotion all in one fell swoop. Plus, he wasn't sure it was any of that soul mate stuff, anyway. He only knew he needed her and cared for her more than he thought was possible after such a short time together. Fate had bound them to the other, and he intended to find out why.

She glowered at him through thick lashes lined with distrust, not that he blamed her. But she looked so darn cute in her constant volleying for the upper hand, he couldn't help but smile.

When she caught his grin, her look lost its hard edge, and her gaze went back to appraising rather than judging. He'd take it.

"Well, do you at least have half an excuse for why you left me out here when the phone call clearly had to do with my safety? I had to take myself on a tour of your home so my brain wouldn't overthink the situation and make it worse. Both situations. You can't keep treating me like a damsel in distress, Gael. Not if you expect to have a relationship."

He went to her and closed his hands around hers, leaving his wine all but forgotten on the counter. Her hands still shook, but they were cool to the touch, and they transferred that chill to Gael. Finally, his internal temperature dropped and he didn't feel like he might spontaneously combust anymore. God, she was good at regulating him, his emotions included. He could only hope to be that for her. Clearly, he had work to do in that department, but that didn't mean he wouldn't die trying.

"I know that. And it won't happen again, Lissa. I promise. The only reason I took the call out of the room is because, for whatever reason, my brain shuts off when I'm with you. Hell, it stops working when I even think about you. All I want to do is rip your clothes from your body and give you the attention you deserve. I was afraid if I was near you, the distraction would prevent me from hearing something crucial about the case back home. That's it, that's the only reason I left. Still, I'll get a hold of my teenage libido when I'm around you. I'm a grown adult in charge of an entire naval force. You wouldn't think it would be that difficult to tell my lower half to calm down and be quiet until my responsibilities were taken care of."

He chuckled, but nothing about this was funny. He really couldn't control his body when Lissa was within a square mile of him, and if only a wall separated them? Ha. All bets were off.

He needed to get a grip. And fast.

Lissa's brows arched up, perfectly manicured rainbows of disbelief. "That's the truth? That's the only reason you left me out here alone?"

Her gaze felt like standing beneath the afternoon summer sun, but it had softened and didn't scorch him the way it had earlier.

"*Dios*, yes. It's the honest truth. I wanted you so bad I was sure I'd get distracted if you were there and miss something important. Something that might save your life. I'd rather have you mad as hell at me than hurt—or worse. That was a risk I couldn't take. Please understand I think of you as more of an equal than I do any of my family. Any of my military brothers or sisters. I just can't lose you."

When a smile broke on her face, it lit up the room as if someone had shined a spotlight on them.

"That's kind of sweet, if not a little nerdy and overprotective."

He chuckled, feeling every bit the geek she thought him to be. As long as she smiled like that at him, he didn't care if she thought he was a goody-two-shoes with his apron strings still attached. Well, maybe not that last part. He'd never been close to his parents, though their disconnect was nothing compared to Lissa's with her folks.

"Whatever it takes to keep you smiling like that, Liss. It's all I've ever wanted since I met you."

A shadow passed over her face but flitted by as quickly as it came again. God, he couldn't wait until he could read those micro-changes in her emotions without her ever having to say a word.

"The truth," she said, and the only reason he heard her was the fact that her cheek was pressed against his ear. The two words came out like a whisper of wind over an open field, slight and almost invisible, as did the five that followed them. "I only want the truth."

"Of course. I'll tell you anything you want to know,

Lissa. I don't want any secrets from you."

Yep, that time he was positive. Something dark moved over her features, but it left before he could call her on it.

"Then tell me everything. Starting with the phone call."

She led the way out of the kitchen, wine glass in hand. He followed her, his own goblet sitting heavy in his palm. She sure knew how to pour a glass of wine that would keep him from needing a refill any time soon. He swelled with pride, watching her make her way to the sitting room at the back of the house as if she'd grown up there. She navigated through the halls easily, just as he'd hoped when he'd designed the home to include her tastes.

When they settled into opposite ends of the leather couch facing the floor-to-ceiling windows, Gael took a minute to appreciate the moment. Lissa's tall, curvy frame was enveloped by the enormous piece of furniture, giving her an almost delicate appearance. To see her beside him, in the home he'd built optimistically for them, it tugged at his chest as if a string connected her to it. She gazed into the pitch blackness in front of them as if it held a secret meant only for her. She seemed a million miles away from him, so he reached out and touched her hand.

It did the job of jostling her from whatever thoughts plagued her, her thin, drawn lips evidence that she wasn't okay with him, though. Not yet.

"I'll bet this is beautiful in the daylight, isn't it?" she almost whispered. She was transfixed by the jet-black screen in front of them. Despite the double-paned glass and thick, insulated walls, they could still hear the storm as its shrill fury screamed and thrashed against all sides of the home. He'd never experienced weather like this here, and the juxtaposition between it and the calm interior had the effect of making the inside space even more safe and welcoming.

"You can't even imagine how stunning. Though not as incredible as the view I have right in front of me."

She glanced over and caught him staring at her. A weak

smile tugged at the corners of her lips. Oh, Lissa. If he didn't find a way to mend the hurt he'd caused her, they might not get back from this. And what a tragedy that would be, especially since it was a simple misunderstanding that caused the fracture in the first place. But her wounds ran deep, and he'd exacerbated them by inadvertently playing into her insecurities.

If only he could show her how much she meant to him. Words wouldn't even be necessary.

As if he summoned the storm to do his bidding, a flash of lightning illuminated the sky and the dramatic landscape in front of them. Of course, he knew the rugged topography in front of them by heart, but the raging winds and rain combined with the snow-covered peaks as steep as any in the Alps made for a formidable scene he knew would impress Lissa.

Lissa gasped as if on cue and jumped into Gael's lap, a tremor coursing through her as he held her tight. It was the physical touch he'd craved, but he couldn't act on it. Not until he was certain of her comfort around him. He would do his best never to take advantage of the trust she placed in him ever again.

"I, um, haven't ever done well with storms," she admitted, and his heart warmed at the confession. "I'm sorry. Between this and the helicopter ride, you must think I'm ridiculous." Still, she made no move to extricate herself from his grasp. He was afraid to breathe in case it shook her free of whatever spell the storm had her in that kept her pressed to him. Her skin was warmer than her grasp had been earlier, but like before, it evened out the chill that her proximity sent racing through him. She was a damn miracle worker when it came to regulating his temperature, his mood, his fears.

Dio. How had he lived without her the past two years?

She feigned a laugh but tensed again when another bolt of lightning crashed closer to the house. He squeezed her tighter to his chest and sent up a silent prayer of thanks to whatever gods were pissy at each other for the opportunity it provided. The only issue with her sitting this close to him was the erection he now had to maneuver around so he didn't scare her off with it.

The outside world shook with anger, but inside, he had everything he'd ever wanted.

"I'll be okay, Gael," she whispered, adjusting slightly so only her leg remained draped over his. "You don't have to shield me from the tough stuff. I can handle the truth, no matter how hard it is to tell me."

Of course, she could. He'd never been in any doubt about that. It was more a matter of how much to tell her this early in their relationship, of spreading it out so he didn't force her to take on his hurts as well. And there were so many of those…

Catching his father with a woman on his staff in his parents' bed.

The debate stage that had been his childhood, persistent anger singing the edges of what should have been a happy childhood filled with the means and love to nourish him and Tomás.

Countless other slights that he still carried with him, but none greater than losing Michelle. When Lissa had shared her experience with losing her sister, he'd known she would understand the loss Michelle had carved into his chest in the exact shape of her small, delicate frame.

But telling her about that, explaining how the only time the hole had come close to filling was when he'd met Lissa? That was so much pressure. Too much. His feelings for this woman ran stronger than any storm, deeper than any crevasse, but they'd come up against an indestructible wall if he pushed her with too much too soon. Of that, he was certain.

But he could share the news Tomás had just passed on. It was a start, a solid foundation on which to build a fortress of solitude for her to feel safe in. More than a start, it was his obligation.

He sighed and let the storm and its luminescence distract him for only a moment more while he gathered his thoughts. She was as still as a marble statue beside him, not even her chest rising and falling with breaths.

"Tomás thinks it was someone inside the palace."

Her sharp intake of breath mirrored his exact response an hour ago when Tomás had first told him. Chills raced across his skin as he recalled Tomás's trepidation and fear. His brother cared what happened to Lissa, even if he didn't care for her in the same way Gael did. No matter what, they were both on the same side when it came to protecting the princess.

The implications of Tomás's discovery were far-reaching and severe. Though he'd never share this with her, it had bought them another week together, something he refused to feel guilty about rejoicing over. Tomás had the unfortunate duty to chase down his leads while Gael got to spend another week with the love of his life in a secluded mountain retreat.

A wave of gratefulness washed over him at how everything had panned out. Sure, it would have been easier if he and Lissa had been honest with each other in the Kelles, but even then, hindsight had been 20/20 when it came to meeting Lissa. On one hand, yes, they would have known the other was their betrothed and been able to skip the two-year gap without the other, but at the same time, it still would have ended in a forced marriage.

It was only after making love to Lissa back at the beach house two days ago that he'd realized what a colossal mistake that would have been. Their attraction would have been crushed under the weight and expectation of a crown and duty. Now, even with the convoluted and unpleasant circumstances, they at least had a chance.

The only aspect of their union he felt remotely guilty about was what it would do to Tomás. His brother didn't deserve to work this hard to end up empty-handed, but he was a survivor. He'd live, and love again, whereas Gael didn't think he would if his life didn't include Lissa.

"Do they have any leads?" Lissa asked, snapping Gael out of his private thoughts.

He nodded. "Unfortunately and fortunately, yes. The bad news is, it looks like it might have been Tomás's childhood best friend, Miguel Perez. According to the guard logs from that evening, there were only three people who used that palace exit around the time the note was discovered, and since the other two were your parents on their way back to Aldonia, it's a pretty cut-and-dry case. The unfortunate part is that he's denying it. Tomás is checking his alibi, but until that checks out, he's the only one on the suspect list."

Lissa frowned, the expression tugging at his chest as he fought for a way to bring her smile back. God, why couldn't he just whisk her away, far from these troubles that kept throwing themselves at her feet? If he could, he wouldn't hesitate in stealing her away, but not until he could guarantee her safety.

"But I don't even know him. Why would he want me dead?"

That was the question plaguing Gael as well. All his time in the military had taught him that a motive—a solid reason for the crime to have been committed—was the only difference between a weak case and an airtight one. Without one, even the most damning forensic evidence against someone was just circumstantial as far as Gael was concerned. What Miguel had was a personal vendetta against the Tomás of their youth, but how that extrapolated to Lissa and the present day remained to be seen. He'd since been a loyal and ardent supporter of the crown, no matter who wore it.

Either way, Gael wasn't convinced either way of his guilt or innocence.

"Miguel loved a mutual friend of theirs, Gabriella, and when she disappeared with her family, he focused his blame on Tomás."

"Oh, no. What happened?" Lissa asked, drawing nearer Gael, her face registering alarm.

"Well, Tomás got into a fight with Gabby's brother that put her family on the wrong side of the crown, so they fled to her mother's homeland in Ireland to cool down and never came home. Miguel blames Tomás not only for her family leaving, but the fact that she dropped all contact with the two friends. I guess Miguel has been writing to her and trying to track her down, but it's just radio silence on her end. Since Miguel's family has been a part of the royal guard for six generations, he stayed on to fulfill his post. Tomás thinks he had both motive and opportunity, but I'm not so sure."

"Has he made threats before?"

Gael shook his head. "No, and that's the thing. As an adult, he seemed to come around to the idea that her silence was her own failing, not my brother's. Miguel has been as staunch a supporter of our family as there is. It doesn't mean there isn't any love lost between the two men, but there's never been a problem. Unless Miguel was acting out a long con, this doesn't make sense."

"Not to me, either. I get that it's awful to lose someone you love, but what would it have to do with me?"

"Another issue I can't wrap my head around. Why after all this time? Tomás has had plenty of girlfriends for Miguel to threaten that he actually liked—no offense to present company—so why harass a woman Tomás just met?"

Lissa nodded along as he spelled out his doubts, but her face didn't register the same concern Geal felt brewing in his chest. If Miguel really was behind this, what would stop him from reaching beyond the castle walls to inflict pain on Tomás through Lissa or her family? Even though there weren't any misgivings of love passed between her and her father, she probably wouldn't want anything to happen to him.

"It doesn't feel right," she said and got up to pace the

space between the couch and coffee table. "I wasn't in the palace longer than a few hours when the letter arrived, and Tomás said my official arrival wouldn't be announced until the following morning. By then, the note had been discovered and you and I were whisked away to the beach. I don't see how Miguel—palace position or not—would have been able to execute such a bold move without being discovered, and so quickly after my secret arrival. Heck, you didn't even know I would be there."

She was right. And she'd given a voice to his concerns. Miguel was a member of the guard so he'd have access to itineraries, and yes, he'd been around the entryway where the note was discovered, but an event as integral to the safety of the country as the meeting of a new family tied to the crown would be kept to one or two high-level security staffers at most.

Miguel wasn't even stationed at the main palace, but the grounds. His family had all served the same post—a post that had neither access nor opportunity to commit the crime Miguel was accused of.

"I know. You're right. I told Tomás the same thing and he has his doubts as well, but right now, there isn't more to go on. There are no fingerprints, no trace forensic evidence at all tying anyone to the letter, just the keypad timestamp."

"Do they have Miguel in custody?"

"They do, but we're bringing your folks back to the palace under our protection just in case someone is frustrated they can't get to you and goes after them instead."

Lissa frowned, likely considering all the new information he'd passed on to her. Her expression became concerned, then grew angry, her bottom lip trembling in the way he'd seen it shake in the Kelles when she briefly talked about having to go home. This new stress was a lot to take in, to process, and damn if he didn't want to just curl up with her and let their bodies talk about anything other than the risk to her life, the throne she was to inherit if he sent her back to Galicia unmarried, or the myriad other problems stalking their happiness and casting a shadow over it.

"Lissa, I'm sorry. This is my family's fault. I understand why you might have doubts about marrying Tomás or myself. But please know I won't let anything happen to you. You're too important to me."

She nodded, but her brows remained pinned together in a frown above her nose. Finally, she gazed up at him, water lining the bottom rims of her eyes, which were the same jade green he'd come to love but with a dense fog covering them, as if something clouded her vision.

"Important enough to tell me the truth?"

Her eyes locked on his, her gaze penetrating and igniting his stomach in a rolling wave of flames that threatened to burn him from the inside out. Why did that look, the one that saw right through to his core, illuminating his depths usually swathed in darkness, frighten him?

"Of course," he assured her. "I'll tell you everything you need to know. Anything, Lissa."

She squinted, her lips and brows tightly drawn together.

"I believe you will. So why don't you start with the girl in the photo on your desk? Tell me why you've been keeping her from me, Gael."

Whatever flames were engulfing Gael's stomach evaporated, turning his center to ice. Anything except *that*. That little girl was off-limits, even to Lissa, at least at that moment.

Why? he lamented. Why did she ask for the one thing he couldn't give her? Because Michelle wasn't his to give. Not yet, not without talking to his family first. Which meant the girl in the photos was the one thing, the one person who could keep Gael from getting what he truly wanted—the girl in front of him.

"I can't, Lissa. Not yet. I have to talk to someone else

before we can have that conversation. I hope you understand."

"I don't. I've told you everything about my life—my neurotic family, the death of my sister. My abusive father. And you can't open up to me about a *photo*? Do you even see the double standard, or are you just so accustomed to getting what you want that you automatically shut down when anyone breaks rank?"

He fell back against the couch cushion as if he'd been shot. Jesus, this woman didn't pull any punches, did she? She wasn't wrong, but still…

Her tone was ice, her scorn palpable. Where had he gone wrong? He hadn't said no, just that he needed time. That wasn't too much to ask, was it?

"Liss, I'll tell you, I promise. I just need to catch my breath and figure out a few things, okay? I mean, you just came back into my life, and while it's everything I've ever wanted, it wasn't exactly an easy reunion. You're engaged to my brother, the future king of Galicia, and someone's out to kill you. All I'm asking for is a chance to get those couple of snags ironed out. Then, we'll talk. Okay?"

There. That wasn't so hard. He'd stood up for himself and shown her he could take care of her at the same time. Because that was his priority, making sure the woman he loved was safe. Then, and only then, could they open up the can of worms that was his dead sibling and the emotional void it had carved out in his chest. A canyon of grief only Lissa had been able to lessen. That she was the only one to have placed a bridge across the gap, fill it with love and the happiest memories he could recall, was a lot of pressure to put on her. Especially when her life was physically in danger.

Baby steps. Save the princess, then spill his emotional trauma at her feet.

If only either of those was as simple as they sounded reverberating against the inside of his skull.

He smiled at her when she didn't reply, wishing they

could go back to where they were a couple of hours ago when they'd arrived, dripping wet and wind-blown, but deliriously happy to find warmth in each other's arms.

She didn't return his smile. Instead, she stood and walked toward the door. Her scarlet curls had dried, cascading down her back in a perfect V that ended at her intoxicating hips. Watching her walk away from him was yet another lesson in duality. On one hand, he'd follow those sashaying hips anywhere they led him. On the other, though, he was well aware her back to him wasn't a sign she was leading him anywhere. It was quite the opposite, actually. She was leaving him, and there wasn't a damned thing he could do to stop her.

When she turned her head at the door, hope surged like electricity in his veins.

"Fine. But I can't and won't marry you with secrets between us, Gael. The wedding is off the table unless you can be honest with me."

He sighed and pinched the bridge of his nose. A migraine knocked on the back of his skull, persistent and inevitable.

"I understand, but my hands are tied where she is concerned. I hope you'll forgive me."

She walked out of the room, leaving her wine and his heart behind. God, he hoped she heard that last part, that he wanted to protect her and save her before adding more pressure to her life. Because if she didn't, he will have lost the only two females in his life who'd ever meant anything to him.

And the last one might be the final blow that killed him.

CHAPTER EIGHT

Lissa stalked the border to her room, corner to corner like a lioness on the prowl. He couldn't tell her, huh? But he still expected her to fall at his feet in gratitude for marrying her and wrenching her free of her father's grasp? Not a chance. Every time she turned on the balls of her feet and stormed in the other direction, a new wave of fury washed over her.

How dare he? He demanded so much of her, challenged her in ways she hadn't asked for, and frankly wasn't sure she appreciated. Yet, when it came time to be challenged by her? Oh, no. All bets were off, and he was back to acting like an injured animal.

As manipulation techniques went, his wounded pride act wasn't as nefarious as some of the nonsense her father had pulled on her, but it was still manipulation, plain and simple. And she wasn't having any of it.

How long—*how long*—was she expected to bow to the wishes of the men in her life, who thought they knew what was best for her? Ha! As if any of them had a clue what she needed, what her happiness looked like or called for.

At least she had the courage to be vulnerable. She'd been eviscerated so many times by those who were supposed to care most for her that she couldn't keep track of the abrasions anymore. And still, she'd shown up for Gael, shared some of her most profoundly intimate hurts—not because she expected him to heal them but because that shared vulnerability was the only way the two of them would ever have a chance.

She snatched a pillow off the impossibly comfortable bed she'd thrown herself onto when she first stormed into the room and screamed into it. It helped, but just in case, she allowed one more feral cry of frustration to pass between her lips before lowering the feather pillow back where it belonged.

Breathing easier, she glanced around the room, taking it in with more care than her first cursory glance of the space she'd made when Gael was tied up in his office, planning her rescue from invisible evil villains. Another slight, another time she'd been shoved to the periphery to watch from the sidelines as her life was orchestrated without her consent.

She barked out a humorless laugh, determined not to let him spoil the rest of the evening. When she'd heard Gael shutting down the house and caught the soft sound of the door next to her shutting, she'd snuck back to the kitchen for some food and replaced her wine while she was there. Now, realizing she was surrounded by more comfort and amenities than her father had in his whole estate, there was no reason she shouldn't enjoy it.

Even if her infuriating host was just like every other man she'd ever met, determined to steal her joy. He had a hero complex, was manipulative as the rest of them, and too damn demanding for his own good. Not to mention closed off to anyone's pain other than his own.

Ugh. Never mind. *Enough about him.*

What about that bathtub she caught a glimpse of on her prowl through the room earlier?

The porcelain tub was grand enough to get Gael out of her mind for a split second as she took in the deep pool with jets lining the oval side panel. And the stained oak bath caddy straddling the edges? A work of genius. It had two circular reliefs cut out of it that would perfectly house either a stemless or long-stemmed wine goblet, and was paired with a water glass holder, a thin, oval relief for her phone, and yes—gift amongst gifts—a book rack to lay open a novel while she soaked.

Oh, yes, this was how she was spending the rest of her night. Soaking and not thinking of the frustrating man who shared the west wall with her. A man who was likely undressing and sliding in between silk sheets wearing nothing but a smile as he had the morning they'd made love.

Good grief. Couldn't she go five minutes without Gael infiltrating her thoughts? In lieu of an answer, she fought against the image of Gael slipping into the tub behind her, using his hands to wash her stomach, her hips, her—

No! Her subconscious reprimanded her. *Forget about him and take care of yourself. Make yourself happy for once. Because, if not, when?*

She forced a mental agreement between her mind and heart, one of them aching as the silent promise was made. She wasn't sure she could keep it, but she'd damn well try.

She grumbled to herself for the umpteenth time since meeting Gael about the failings of falling for a man when she didn't have her heart to give. She turned on the tub faucet, testing the water before letting the near-boiling liquid fill the tub. Steam wound around her like a serpent as she slipped out of her sweater and tights. As she set up her wine, retrieved a book from her carry-on bag, and filled a glass with water, questions began to surface in her mind like bubbles.

Who is that little girl, and who does he have to talk to in order to share her with me?

What would it take to get Gael to open up to me? Really open up the way I need him to?

One question shoved the others out of the way and

was louder than all the rest.

What will I do if he can't?

The question, and its as-of-yet-unattainable answer, fell from her head, settling heavily over her heart. She'd come so far with Gael since meeting him two years ago and wasn't sure at this point she'd be able to let him go. At least not as easily as she imagined she'd be able to leave him when they'd first met. The man was supposed to be a fling, and yet it had taken less than three days to complete a hostile takeover of her heart.

Had she been aware of the lasting effects of her decision to seduce him—for them both—she might not have pursued it at all. A few nights of unabashed freedom and intimacy weren't worth the hell she'd created in each of their lives.

Her pulse raced. Her heart recognized her unspoken words as the lies they were almost instantly. The idea she could have walked away from Gael wasn't true, not a word of it. Ugh. Honestly, there wasn't a force on earth that could have kept her from Gael once she'd laid eyes on him. Her body was a magnet pulled toward his, her skin an electric charge that ignited when he was in proximity. When he touched her? She was aflame, unable to douse the inferno he caused in her.

No, loving Gael was a foregone conclusion, but it stood to reason she could only love him so long as he was able to love her back, right? Or, even if he didn't, and she kept on loving him against the will of her mind, she couldn't stay with him knowing he didn't reciprocate her feelings.

The thing was, until that evening, she'd been pretty dang certain he felt the exact same way about her as she did about him. They more than cared for each other—it was love, plain and simple. How else could they explain the passion they shared, the sacrifices they were willing to make to continue building a life together?

Except she'd found the line he wouldn't cross, hadn't

she? The photo of the little girl, the mystery female standing between them. What did he think would happen if he told Lissa he was a father, that if they married she'd be a stepmother? That she'd bolt without sitting down to talk with him first? Because of the way he reacted to her question, it seemed as if he wasn't giving her the benefit of the doubt, that he didn't trust her with his heart and his family.

A startling realization crashed into Lissa's chest as she slid into the tub, relishing the liquid heat that engulfed her tired body. *He has to speak to the girl's mother.*

Of course—it made perfect sense why he'd put that conversation above Lissa's inquiry. In fact, had he not been so responsible, she would have been concerned. She'd expect the same if she shared custody of a child with someone, the dignity and respect of being asked before someone new entered their lives.

Okay. As the wine warmed her from the inside, the water matching the heat on her skin, she exhaled her worries with the breath she'd been holding in. She could wait and give him the time he needed to handle his family issues. Stress lifted off her, carried away with the steam.

She sank lower in the water, letting the restorative power of the bath, the superb wine, and the sounds of the still-raging storm lull her into a sense of peace she hadn't been able to capture in months, years even.

When someone knocked, she responded, "Come in," automatically, her eyes still closed and her body still in repose. She didn't give a thought to Gael's staff coming in while she was in such a vulnerable position. God knew she'd gotten used to being constantly surrounded by palace staff and guards growing up.

Her father had her tailed around the clock when she'd returned from the Kelles, clearly considering her a flight risk, which would have derailed his masterful plan to marry her off before his funds ran out and King Robert cut him off for good. She hadn't been without a guard in two years, so why should things be any different now?

When whoever walked into the room cleared their throat, though, Lissa shot up like a cannon out of the bubble-coated layer of safety the water provided her. She knew that particular brand of throat clearing as if she'd heard it every day of her life.

Gael. Oh, damn.

Suddenly, her matted hair and exposed flesh were all too conspicuous. She may be used to staff always around, flitting in and out of her periphery so much that they usually passed by unnoticed, but Gael was not included in that group. Every time he was within six feet of her, the hairs on her forearm stood on end and her heart pattered out a beat that said, "There he is! The only person on the planet to make me feel like this!"

Gael inspired a visceral reaction that she couldn't hide fully clothed on a good day. But naked and resembling a drowned poodle? Ha! He could probably see the wanting on every cell bared to him—which was expansive to say the least.

She crossed her arms over her now-exposed breasts and slid back beneath the bubbled surface, her cheeks burning in a way that had nothing to do with the scalding water. Damn her Irish skin for showing off each of her emotions like an emotional MRI.

At least he didn't appear to be unfazed either.

The hungry gaze raking over her body from top to cherry-painted toes was almost slate gray with emotion. If she read him right, it reflected a lust and desire that she mirrored as she took in the man standing before her.

He'd shed his light jacket and stood before her barefoot in jeans and a loose cotton tee that fit as snugly as if it were designed around his sculpted torso. Christ, he was gorgeous, even dressed as casually as he was. Or perhaps especially because of his informal attire. There was something provocative and alluring seeing him without his proverbial military suit of armor. It evened the playing field a little, Gael stripped down to being just a man, not a prince nor captain.

"I, um…" he began, then cleared his throat again.

She bit the inside of her cheek to keep from laughing at his nervousness. Did his confidence fly the coop with the service medals and awards?

Except the way he licked his lips and left them gleaming with moisture she wanted pressed against her skin meant none of this was funny. Her smile evaporated, replaced with a cavernous ache that only this man had ever inspired in her.

"I didn't know you'd be awake still. You had quite a day."

"And yet you knocked anyway."

That observation knocked his usual self-confidence off-kilter even more, and his gaze fell from hers to the floor, where her black lace panties lay discarded at his feet. This time, she let a small giggle escape as he fought for a place to land his gaze that wouldn't scream *There's a naked woman you've slept with right in front of you!* When he settled on his hands shoved in his jeans, his gaze stuck on the ceiling, she had to bite her tongue to keep from teasing him.

"I heard some muffled noise and was worried. I'm sorry I interrupted your, um, your bath."

"It's fine. I'm actually glad you stopped by. Can we talk?" Her stomach fluttered underwater. Talking was the last thing she wanted to do with this delectable man just feet in front of her. And while she was already disrobed as well. But talking was a necessary evil if they hoped to be more than a fleeting, passionate affair.

"Of course. Give me just a moment." He walked out of the bathroom, and his absence did more to unnerve her than his presence did. Was he fetching her robe so he wouldn't have to contend with the distraction her bare flesh posed? After what seemed an eternity, he arrived with the desk chair from the bedroom, which he set beside the tub. The small reprieve from the bathroom seemed to allow some of his fortitude to come back. He sat, his elbows firm on his knees, his chin resting on his fists. How was it possible that with every gesture he made, he grew more and more attractive? "Okay, tell me what's on your mind, *cariña*."

She warmed at the endearment. "Thank you, Gael."

He faltered, one of his elbows slipping and jostling his torso and confidence again. Clearly, he hadn't expected her gratitude.

"For what? I've been closed off and kept you at arm's length. What could you possibly have to thank me for?"

"For so much. For keeping me safe, for offering up your home and your time. I'm well aware babysitting duty is far beneath your skills, and I've been less than grateful for what you've given up. So... thank you."

Was he blushing? "You're welcome. And it isn't beneath me. Whatever you may think of me for keeping you in the dark about certain issues, I've only ever wanted your safety and happiness. That I might be a part of both is an honor I wasn't sure I'd get after you walked out of my room that morning in the Kelles."

Her heart pounded against her chest loud enough that she worried he'd hear the echo reverberate against the tile walls.

"I know. Me neither. And I can wait to know who the girl in the photo is. I'm sorry I rushed you. But I do need to talk to you about something else that's been bothering me."

"Anything." He reached out and cupped her shoulder with his hand, sending a jolt of heat racing through her veins.

She inhaled deeply, her fortitude wavering under his penetrating gaze and loving touch. All she wanted to do was jump the poor man, but that wouldn't get them where either of them wanted to be. There would be time for that if she could just get the courage to talk to him.

"It all comes down to the fact that I can take care of

myself, Gael. That's been the most frustrating part of the past week since I arrived in Spain, that yo"ve been treating me like a damsel in distress that needs saving from a white knight or not at all. Remember the woman you met in the islands? Remember how she could take care of herself, if not take on some fights on behalf of others?"

He nodded, his head bowed and cheeks flushed. He most likely hadn't ever been admonished by anyone other than his direct superiors in the Navy, and wasn't used to a verbal dressing down. Well, he'd better get used to it if he kept up his savior complex. Because that was not who she was, nor who she wanted to be. She wanted an equal love, one where she wasn't told who to be or how to live by yet another male in her life.

"Well, she's still here. *I'm* still here, and I'm the same independent woman you claim you fell in love with. So, why won't you treat me like you treated the woman you met in the Kelles? Your behavior since we met at the palace is exactly why I didn't tell you who I was back then, don't you see that? Everyone I meet who finds out I'm a member of the royal family—and which royal family— wants to save me from my father, save me from the marriage he's resigned me to, save me from the royal life I want no part of. But the only one who can actually do that is me."

"I know," Gael sighed. His chest heaved, and a quick draw of his breath captured her attention.

She'd hurt him again. But she'd stood up for herself, and no small measure of pride blossomed in her chest. The guilt of that pride coming at the cost of Gael's wounded sense of gallantry was still there—honestly, she wondered if she'd ever become strong enough to step out of her father's shadow and overcome that repentant side of her personality. But it wasn't as pervasive as it had been. She was growing up and becoming the woman she'd tried to be regardless of her less-than-ideal circumstances.

"Then what do we do about that?" she asked. It wasn't

a rhetorical question. She genuinely wanted to know how they moved past Gael's flagrant disregard of her independence and got back to who they were in the islands, secrets notwithstanding.

A wicked gleam passed over his face, and the water, which had begun to cool to room temperature, suddenly seemed to boil around her as the heat from her center flushed her skin. Good Lord, he was as mouth-watering as the rarest filet, scrumptious as the most decadent sliver of dark chocolate. She'd gladly give up both for eternity if he would keep looking at her like that. His hand slipped down to her chest, his fingers splayed over her collarbone. Okay, she'd never eat anything other than brown rice and broccoli if he'd keep touching her that way.

"If we want to get back to who we were in the Kelles, we should start where we left off there. As I recall," he said, standing tall over her and tugging his shirt over his head, "you were dressed, and I wasn't wearing a thing when you walked out on me. Though, I think I like you better like this."

Her stomach flipped over itself and sent a rogue wave of lust careening over her as he stepped out of his jeans as well. She licked her lips. There he was, clad only in snug, black boxer briefs that reminded her of one very obvious reason she'd been unable to walk out on Gael after the first night they'd slept together.

The man was built like a Greek statue brought to life for her pleasure only.

Of course, his kindness, attentive hands and lips, and arresting smile that shone down on her brighter than the island sun didn't dissuade her from crashing headlong into love with him when it should have been a weekend of fun to keep her warm on lonely nights. It had been that, as well, yet she'd also never forgotten the man who'd been the cause of those memories, and no man had come close to measuring up since.

All of that—the past, her memories, their

unconventional start—slid from her consciousness, drowning in the water that surrounded her. It was time to make new memories, starting now, as the man she loved with all her heart and every cell of her eager body pulled her out of the tub, not bothering to dry her off. He carried her to the bed and laid her out on full display for him. When her burning gaze clashed with his, she welcomed the future that stood in front of her with open arms.

Hours later, physically sated and emotionally restored, Lisa's eyes fluttered open at the same time a barrage of images flashed across her vision. Gael's steady hands making fast work of her skin, her needs, her burgeoning desire. His muscled torso and sculpted arms bracing himself above her as he loved her with a tenderness she'd never experienced. The exaltation of him collapsing beside her, as seemingly depleted as she was. And then she'd fallen into the deepest sleep she'd had in months. God, loving him was worth that alone, but he hadn't stopped at making her feel safe enough to sleep without one eye on the door, on who might be waiting around the corner to disturb her tranquility.

No, he'd made sure she enjoyed every minute of earning that safety.

She bit back a grin. What she'd asked for was a recollection of what they'd been like together in the Kelles and how he thought of her as a woman. What she got was a devoted and driven man bent on making sure no other lover, past or future, would come close to fulfilling her the way he did. Gael had been a man on a mission, his singular purpose to love her into oblivion.

And he had, oh how he had.

But speaking of the man, where was he now? The left side of the bed was made up as if he'd never slept—and not slept—next to her. The rest of the house was as still as the eye of a hurricane, the storm abating sometime during her slumber. The shades were drawn so she couldn't see what beautiful havoc it'd wrecked on the rugged landscape surrounding Gael's secret fortress. It was likely as stunning as the beach, just not her normal taste in scenery.

She stretched, sighing as life flooded her limbs. A hint of pine and holly filled her nostrils, reminding her of the impending holiday looming on her horizon. For the first time in her life, she wasn't dreading spending Christmas with someone, especially because of the particular someone she was holed up in the middle of nowhere with. In fact, excitement surged through her now-invigorated veins, anticipation about what their life could look like making her dizzy. The world was open to them as soon as they married.

After last night, she didn't have a doubt in her mind marrying Gael was what her heart desired. Sure, they had some challenges ahead, but what couple didn't? With him, she could be her authentic self and not worry about letting someone down. With him, she could finally escape the oppressive thumb her father had her pinned under. With Gael, her future expanded rather than contracted as it had for her life until this point.

Last night made her desire for more not only okay, but right. She couldn't help the smile that played on her lips.

Yet, as much as she wished she could lie in comfort the rest of the morning, seducing Gael into a repeat performance of last night, she had to find him and figure out what dragged him out of bed before dawn. Something had happened, that was certain. There was no way on earth the Gael of last night would have left her side without at least waking her with a kiss, if not something more... carnal.

She slipped her legs from beneath the covers, only to have them wrapped instantly in a frigid chill not unlike being submerged in an ice bath. Oh, yeah, they definitely weren't on the coast in Galicia anymore. In fact, she'd never missed the temperate Aldonian winters until that moment. She shivered and scanned the room for her tights. The almost oppressive arctic air showed her yet another benefit to cuddling up beside Gael and not leaving the comfort of the down comforter until noon, but that wasn't in the cards.

Tracking down her perpetually elusive paramour was.

She tugged on her tights, her teeth still chattering, and then threw open the drapes. *Whoa....* He wasn't kidding when he said that particular location in the Pyrenees was magical. A thick blanket of snow was draped delicately over the most rugged, sweeping mountain range she'd ever seen, the whole scene framed by thin, pink clouds that looked watercolored in place. Majestic didn't begin to cover it. This place was pure perfection, even if it was freezing.

There wasn't a soul around—no one to tell her where to go, what to do.

Just as she stepped away from the window, a smile still pinned to her face, a subdued voice rose in pitch behind the bedroom door. It sounded angry and frustratingly familiar.

What the—

A tingling sensation she recognized as fear crept up her spine and tickled her throat.

Something was off.

She tiptoed over, cringing when the wooden floor creaked under her movement. The voice grew quieter, but it was unmistakable. It belonged to the same man who'd loved her within an inch of her life last night, whispering intimacies meant only for her ears. Now, that voice was shouting in hushed whispers, the words not as discernable as the anger carried on them.

Why was he making secret calls again when he'd promised her a partnership, when he'd sworn transparency? How—*how*—was she supposed to trust him when every other moment he was stealing himself away to make frantic calls and orchestrate her future on her behalf? Just when she thought she'd made headway in her life, with the men in it, the one person she trusted most pulled this?

Anger rolled inside her like a swarm of hornets, caustic and deadly. She backed away from the door just as the voice silenced and the door opened, and she attempted a last-minute adjustment of her sweater as if she hadn't just been eavesdropping.

Before she met his gaze, she fixed hers with the million-dollar smile and thousand-yard stare she'd perfected for when she dealt with her manipulative, dangerous father. The look that said *What can I help you with,* dear, albeit laced with poison.

"Good morning," he coughed out, his voice gruff but not as livid as it had been seconds before.

"I thought so. Now, I'm not so sure." She was done pussy-footing around Gael. He could either give it to her straight or not at all. The promise she'd exacted from him still stood as far as she was concerned. If only holding him accountable didn't come just hours after holding him in her arms.

"I know. I'm sorry. I got a call early this morning and didn't want to wake you."

"Oh, I'm sure you didn't," she spat out, aware the anger she released with every breath was landing square on the chest of the man she loved. What was worse was how powerless she was to stop it. She'd reached her capacity for duplicity and deviousness from the men in her life. "But I'm awake now."

He sighed, a deep exhale that matched the resignation on his pursed lips. When had those bags appeared under his eyes? He was still startlingly handsome, but he looked worn down, defeated. So was she, though, and becoming more so by the minute.

"I see that. Elisabeth, can I talk to you a minute?" he asked.

Elisabeth? What was she, a stranger all of a sudden? Her thoughts were spiraling, imagining how they got from last night to here in less than a heartbeat. The other shoe, the one she was perpetually worried about dropping, seemed perilously close to falling out of her grasp.

Gael's gaze was pinned to the hazy sky behind her, his hands shoved deep in his pockets. Her heart sank even further into the pit of her chest. Of course. She knew why he was there. Just as she'd talk herself into marrying him, he'd come to break it off. She'd dug in too deep, demanded too much too fast, and scared him away. Not that she blamed him, of course, but it would be comical how off sync they were if it weren't so agonizing.

"What is it?" Her voice cracked along the seams, breaking open the flood of fear that had been all but forgotten in the pit of her stomach until that moment.

How could she be so foolish as to assume that because she'd been happy—really, genuinely happy—for perhaps the first time in her life, that it would last? Her heritage seemed to demand the opposite from her. The moment she'd been born into her father's home—an only child once her sister fled for safety only to be killed for the sin of escaping a tyrant's rule—she'd known she'd be responsible for creating her own happiness. Even then, she was aware it would be fleeting.

"I have to talk to you, but I don't have a damned clue where to start."

"I've never been one for beating around the bush. Just tell me, Gael. I can handle it." As soon as the lie escaped her lips, a shiver ran through her limbs. The only thing she couldn't handle was him telling her goodbye.

"Your father. The threat. It's… He's…" Gael paced the bedroom, growing more agitated with every pass he made.

Lissa's blood turned to ice, freezing her in place. Her father? What about him? It wasn't good. Gael's demeanor said that more than his words.

"What? Was he hurt?" There was no love lost between her and her father, but he was still family, and the idea that he'd be injured, or worse, because of her was too difficult to consider.

"No. He's fine, physically anyway." He paused, seeming to consider how much to tell her. Finally, he continued, though the moment he did, she immediately wished he hadn't. "Tomás found him halfway through piecing together another letter, this time with a monetary demand attached. But it's more *what* he said when Tomás confronted him."

"Wait, go back. My father was making a ransom note?"

"He was. On behalf of someone else, he claims. Though all evidence seems to contradict that…" He trailed off, his square jaw set with the exception of a small muscle twitch that belied an underlying anger.

No. He wasn't right. He couldn't be. Her father? He wouldn't put himself in the middle of this. Not for all the money in the world. Yet as soon as she exonerated him in her mind, she felt the truth course through her like poison in her veins.

Yes, he would, especially if it meant saving his own skin. In fact, hadn't he been doing just that her whole life? And for far less than all the money in the world?

Still, she needed the words to come from his mouth.

"Gael, you're stalling. Tell me exactly what's going on. I can handle it."

When Gael met her gaze, she wasn't actually sure she could handle what he was about to tell her after all. Hurt lined his eyes, and the bags under them were red as if he'd been crying. Not in all the time she'd known him, which in retrospect hadn't been that long, had she seen him this distraught. Worry tickled her skin.

"Your father was caught in the act of piecing together a ransom note exactly like the one we found outside the castle a week ago. My father brought him in for questioning, and he swore he was acting out orders from someone else, someone who threatened him to go public about his financial ruin if he didn't comply. He wept, Lissa."

"Well, find whoever the person is and haul them in. Who cares if they share my father's financial ruin with the public? It isn't a state secret. Even his cousin, King Robert, has cut him off. My father has no business getting involved, and look at the mess he's made in the process…"

"Lissa," Gael started, cutting her off. The gravity in that one word shut her up from speaking any further. She froze, watching his agitation reach frantic heights. The tension between them was palpable, like the heat in the south mid-summer.

"What? What aren't you telling me?"

"It's you, Lissa. He said he's making the letters at your request so you can get whatever money you think you're owed. It would explain why you 'found' the first letter. I don't want to believe it, but nothing else makes sense. Please tell me I'm wrong. Make me believe you."

Lissa felt like she'd been kicked square in the chest. She couldn't draw in a breath. Her chest was so tight, and her vision faltered, growing fuzzy along the edges.

"You're wrong. Plain and simple. That you could imagine me capable of this for a moment is as close as you've come to being like my father."

"You don't have anything to say other than I'm like him? What about you? Didn't you tell me you'd do anything to get out from under his iron fist?"

"No. No, that's not right. Gael. You know damn well I don't care about the money. I only want my freedom."

"Exactly. But at what cost? Do you want it enough to use force to get out of your father's grasp?"

Wait. He really and truly thought she was capable of this? Like, actually capable of faking a death threat to get out of her debt-ridden family? Yet, as she considered the lunacy behind the idea, she wouldn't put it past someone in her position, either. She had nothing to lose and everything to gain. If—and this was what she needed desperately to convince Gael of before her fate was sealed—she wanted any of that.

The money, the fame, the title…

Yes, she wanted out. Yes, she wanted to be free of her marital obligations, of her father's tyranny. But in no way could she stoop to the depths Gael was accusing her of. That he thought her even remotely guilty was more damning than her father's accusation, which she hadn't even had time to process.

She was speaking quicker now, in a defeated last attempt to convince him of her innocence. His question, the fact that he had to ask at all, spoke to the guilt he'd already assigned her.

"Besides, why would I involve the man who's squandered all of his money when I was supposedly about to marry into a bucket load of it? Does any of that make sense to you?"

She wanted to add, "And I love you. Isn't that enough to earn an acquittal?" But it wouldn't be enough. She knew that as sure as she knew she was losing the battle over her freedom by the look in Gael's eyes. Hurt and betrayal simmered there beneath suspicion. Why should he believe her when it was her father—her very convincing father— and his word against hers?

Again, the truncated time she'd known Gael flaunted itself in front of her, teasing her with all it left open to interpretation. He didn't know her, just as she didn't truly know him. Hell, he was still hiding a secret from her that could make her run for the hills, so who was to say she wasn't doing the same?

"I wish I could believe you. If only you'd told me the truth, Lissa. But you hid it from me and now I don't know who to believe, dammit. Don't you know how much that stings? That I had to hear it from my brother, your future husband?"

The truth? What is he talking about? Lissa had been nothing but forthcoming about her father, his shortcomings, her sister and how she'd walked out on her family years earlier. She'd spilled her secrets at his feet, hoping they were safe in his hands. What could he be talking about?

"I don't know what you're talking about, Gael. I've told you everything, more than I've ever shared with another human being, including my sister."

"See? When I give you the chance to come clean, you can't even talk to me! It's just us, Lissa. Tell me the truth, or I swear, I'll take you back and let them question you themselves."

Her heart beat furiously against her chest like a feral beast trying to tear through its chains. Her skin felt hot, as if it might ignite in flames at the slightest of exhales from Gael.

"Please. I don't know what you want from me," she cried. Tears fell hot and heavy on her cheeks, staining her with the fear she'd kept pent up inside her until now. They were all she had left to give him, but it wasn't what he wanted. That, like so much of him, remained hidden behind his own veil of pain and accusation.

"I want to hear from you about how you're adopted, not even of royal lineage. You faked it along with your family to save them from ruin. Just like you faked the letter you 'found.' I loved you enough not to care, Lissa, but lying about it? I can't forgive that."

He walked out of the room, leaving her to pick up the pieces of her shattered heart. It wasn't watching Gael walk away from her that stung as much as, once again, finding out her life had been a lie. Every last bit. And per usual, she was the last to know.

Of course, she was adopted. How could she not be? It made so much sense she wondered why she hadn't figured it out before Gael's damning last words to her. With her fiery hair and personality to match? Her tall stature and prominent cheekbones? They were all as out of place as she felt at that moment. As she'd been her whole life. She didn't belong anywhere, did she? She was a lie told to get her father what he wanted, and the cost had been great when that lie was discovered.

Too bad she was the one left with the bill. Again.

The door slammed on her and the future she'd so delicately believed in. Gael's footsteps could be heard echoing down the corridor to his room, where his door slammed with equal force.

That was it then. They were over. Just like that.

And that was when it happened.

The other shoe dropped, fractured at her feet, irreparable and ugly in its pieces as if it had been made of glass. If only she was a fairy-tale princess whose happily ever after still awaited her beyond this crushing pain.

Brava, she wanted to scream into the void between her and her father. *Brava*. For he had finally and irrevocably succeeded in destroying what was left of her life.

CHAPTER NINE

Gael gazed out over the precipitous landscape below him, the majesty of it all passing by him. Because how could anything be as breathtaking as having the woman he loved beside him in bed, naked and curled up against the curve of his body like she'd been hours earlier? When he discovered the woman he loved wasn't the woman he thought she was, how was he supposed to find beauty in anything again?

Hell, it had taken a Herculean feat of strength not to torch the home he'd built with them in mind as they left that morning. The only thing saving the structure from a demise as thorough as the obliteration of his heart was that he'd need a safe haven to escape to when his world came crashing down on him in a few hours' time.

The imminence of that moment almost crippled him. Seconds passed by without so much as a warning, bringing him closer to his own destruction. Not only would he have to share with his brother what had transpired between him and Lissa—including their time in the islands—he would have to say goodbye to the only woman he'd ever loved or would again. She was it for him, plain and simple. That it hadn't worked out between them didn't change anything.

He sighed out all the resignation he'd trapped in his chest. A long life of military service lay ahead of him, the only thing he had to look forward to. Well, at this rate, he'd make general before he was forty, especially considering he was going to throw himself into work in a futile attempt to forget about the woman sitting next to him, silently staring out the window of the helicopter.

She'd ignored him since that evening when he'd given her one final chance to come clean. Instead of either denying the accusations he pelted her with, or admit to lying, she'd done the unexpected and thrown the interrogation back on him.

"How dare you accuse me of keeping secrets when you won't tell me who's in that photo. What the hell were you doing discussing my life without me? Again! After we just discussed me being a partner in our decisions, especially where it concerns my health and safety."

And of course he'd acted like a world-class schmuck and replied that his family was none of her business, not anymore. He wasn't proud of it, but dammit if she didn't know just what buttons of his to push. The injured look on her face gave him a moment's pause about whether or not he should be dragging her back into the lion's den, but she had to answer for her crimes. Lying about her heritage being the most egregious of them as far as he was concerned.

The rest of the flight went that way—her silence laced with hostility and him sitting there wondering what he'd done wrong. By the time they landed in Galicia, Gael's head might as well have been on backward. He was no longer confident he was doing the right thing. In fact, a growing sense of dread crept up the back of his neck, erupting his skin in chills.

What if they'd been played? Had he really given Lissa a fighting chance to share her side of things? Or just steamrolled her into admitting what he'd wanted her to admit? He'd all but told her she was guilty in his eyes no matter what, so when she'd offered up protestations, he'd waved her off with the flick of his wrist like the pompous royal he'd never wanted to become. God, he was as bad as his father, wasn't he?

The million-dollar question, though, was if she was at all like hers.

As the wheels touched down, Tomás and three guards came running toward them. Tomás had a bounce in his step that suggested he was a helluva lot happier than Gael was.

"Are those the men who're going to take me to whatever holding cell you have?" Lissa asked. Her voice was distant, cold. She may as well have been back in the chalet for how far she felt from him.

The idea of her chained to a bedpost in a cold, stone room with no windows crushed the last of Gael's resolve into dust.

He nodded, not sure he could trust his own voice.

"Very well. No matter how this pans out, Gael, I'll still always be glad you came back into my life. I'm just sorry you don't feel the same."

I do! he screamed inside his head, but by then, she was out the door, ducking to avoid the blades, escorted by the palace's finest. Where she went, what she did, who she spoke to—none of it was up to him anymore. He'd lost the chance to know anything about her future when he'd refused to listen to her about her past.

The loss hit him across the chest with the force of being pummeled by a prizefighter. He'd been careless, and now he paid the price.

He couldn't wallow too long, though. Tomás was standing there, a smug smile on his face as Gael disembarked. Heat from the tarmac swirled around him, thawing him from the frigidity of the flight home in more ways than one.

"Why do you look so self-satisfied?" Gael asked, pleased to see his brother no matter the challenges that stood as formidable as a stone wall in front of them.

"Because we figured it out, and because you owe me for dealing with Papá the past two weeks."

"Oh, yeah? Well, fill me in. God knows I'd like to know what the hell's been going on around here while I've been relegated to radio silence." He wasn't trying to be cruel, but he felt like a kid carted off to boarding school only to come home on holiday to find out his whole life had been upended.

"I was trying to fill you in while you were still with her, but we couldn't reach you. Why didn't you answer your phone?"

"We've been in the air, Tomás. At your request that we return immediately. Why? What could possibly have changed in the two hours we didn't have service? Surely it couldn't have gotten worse."

Tomás laughed. "That depends on who you are. For Lissa's dad? Yeah. I'd say it got worse. It looks like Lissa's off the hook, though."

Gael's stomach churned like he'd downed a glass of milk well past its expiration date.

What the—? Dio.

"Sorry? Did you say she's off the hook?"

"Seems that way. Her mom came clean, spilled all the family secrets and about a gallon of tears, too. It was a bloody trainwreck, Gael. This family's got more drama than any American reality TV show I've seen, that's for sure. Marrying into it seems a little like a fool's errand. Luckily, the poor girl's about to get another bit of bad news. Not only has her father—well, her adopted father as it turns out—hung her out to dry, but there's no way Papá's touching this family with a six-foot lance, especially not if the princess isn't a royal after all. Worst part is, Elisabeth never knew she wasn't his kid. What a mess." Tomás shook his head. "So, it looks like more of the single life for me. Now I gotta go let Elisabeth know what's going on before she freaks out thinking she's still on trial.

Can you handle processing her dad with the guards? He's here until we can figure out how to charge him."

Gael nodded, an empty gesture. Could he handle such a menial task when he'd managed to mess everything else up?

"What about her mother?"

Tomás shrugged. She's heading home to Aldonia to try to pick up the pieces of her family with King Robert. She didn't know about the letters, but I suspect she's got some explaining to do with her daughter."

"Mmmm," Gael said, his mind already moving past this conversation and trying to pick up the pieces of a life he'd shattered for no reason other than his stubborn refusal to be wrong, to let anyone past his defenses. Damn his father for training him to be nothing other than a stone-cold jerk to the woman he loved.

"Good. Glad to have you back, brother. Wish me luck breaking up with my fiancée."

Tomás chuckled and slapped his brother hard on the back, but Gael didn't budge. He was pinned in place by an overload of information he couldn't process fast enough.

Lissa's dad was behind the whole thing.

She wasn't a royal by blood, so she wouldn't be betrothed to anyone else.

She hadn't lied to him. Which meant she was alone, struggling to make sense of her childhood, likely wondering who her birth father was.

The last realization he had as his brain struggled to catch up to his racing heart was that he'd screwed up. Big time. *God*, he thought as he ran his hands through his hair, pulling at the base of the strands in frustration. *I ruined everything. Everything.* She'd been telling the truth, and he'd treated her like a criminal. If there was a prize for the daftest idiot in the country, he'd be on the short list for certain.

His second thought was how he could fix it this late in the game. Because the last words he'd spoken to Lissa had

155

been laced with hatred and distrust—the same vitriol her family had been spoon-feeding her throughout her life.

Now, it was up to him to pull out all the same stops he'd laid down and throw himself at her feet, swearing never to put her through that again. He'd give her the benefit of the doubt no matter how worried he was about putting himself out there, how scared he was to get hurt. Hadn't she shown enough times over that she'd never hurt him? And yet all he'd given her in return was doubt and trepidation.

Not anymore. He'd lost her twice by not telling her the truth, and dammit—he wouldn't let another chance to love her honestly and completely pass him by.

He jogged after his brother, the exertion waking him up from the trance he'd been in the last twenty-four hours. There was one thing he had to do before he told her everything, starting with who the mystery girl was in the photo. It was time to fill his brother in on who Lissa was and what she meant to him and hope his brother understood there was no way Gael was letting her go again.

"Wait," Gael called after Tomás, who'd barely made it twenty feet before being stopped by an advisor. "I need to talk to you before you go to Papá. There's something you should know, something I should have told you a while ago." Met with a concerned look from his brother, he started at the beginning and didn't hold anything back.

An hour later, Tomás stared at Gael, a look on his face that matched how Gael felt. Something like being pummeled by a bull and dragged behind it for a few kilometers.

"*Mierda*, brother. You really stepped in it, didn't you?" Tomás asked.

"That's an understatement. I feel more like I got stepped on."

"So, she's been the one you've been after this whole time? It figures. I thought I felt something between you two when I went to check on her that night you two left, but I didn't have a clue what I was missing, did I?"

"No, and I'm sorry about that, *hermanito*."

"Oh, well. I can see why you're into her. She's like one of those mermaids that sucks sailors into the sea with all that red hair and sass."

"A siren."

"Yeah, that's the one. She wrapped her tentacles around you, didn't she?"

Gael nodded as a smile crept up his cheeks. "Mixing metaphors, are we? Anyway, the problem is, I don't know what to do to fix any of it. With you, with Papá, but most of all with Lissa."

Tomás, ever the optimist, smiled and let a small peal of laughter pass through his pursed lips.

"Well, I can't say anything about Papá or Lissa, but you're square with me. Heck, I wish you'd told me before your little adventure. I wouldn't have bugged you with all the blackmail updates. God knows after the way you've been pining after this woman for two years, you could have used some time together. At least through Christmas. Speaking of, you gotta let me see this place of yours, *hermano*. It sounds spectacular."

"It is. I actually designed and built it with her in mind. Isn't that crazy? I mean, I'd only known her for three days when I did that, and I kept the plans moving full steam ahead when I hadn't been able to locate her after all that time. I should be committed."

"That's love, Gael. We've all got to be a little crazy if we're going to dive into something so dependent on someone else's happiness. At least you found it, though. Look at Mamá and Papá. They're still searching and they're twice our age. My advice?" Tomás asked.

Gael let loose a laugh of his own at the idea of taking his perpetually single brother's advice. Still, he nodded. He didn't care where the assist came from if it helped him win her back.

"Go tell her everything you just told me. Tell her you love her, tell her about Michelle, and for God's sake, let her in. There's no halfway when it comes to love."

Gael's bottom jaw unhinged, leaving him gaping at his younger brother.

"Since when did you get so smart?" Gael asked. Just like when Tomás had taken on the role of crowned prince, he seemed to have grown up and matured overnight. A swelling of pride filled the cavernous hole Lissa had left in his chest.

"Since you left to see the world and found the love of your life. I realized I wanted that, too, and now, thanks to you, I just might get it."

"Papá's going to let you marry outside your birthright?"

Tomás nodded. "I don't think he wants another fiasco like this one on his hands. He's too old for this kind of drama. Speaking of, why don't you let me handle telling him about all this while you track down that woman of yours?"

"I don't deserve you, Tomás."

"No, you don't, but I'll let you stick around anyway. Seriously, Gael. Don't let her go without a fight. I did that with Rebecca and not a day goes by that I don't regret it."

"The woman from Georgia?"

"Another story for another time. Go get Lissa back and don't stop until she knows how you feel."

"I won't. And thanks again, Tomás. I'm proud of you, you know."

Tomás shook his head and waved Gael away. "Get out of here before I change my mind and have you tell Papá on your own while I sit back with a bag of churros and watch the fireworks. You know, without your drama, it's going to get awfully boring around here."

"Isn't that a good thing?" Gael laughed. Tomás nodded his agreement and gathered his jacket to head into the palace alongside his brother.

Honestly, Gael couldn't wait for his life to get boring if

he had any say in it. Well, perhaps not boring, but at least without the peaks and valleys of emotions he and Lissa had experienced lately. He wanted to settle down with her in the south of Spain—as far from the royal *circo* as he could get them and still be close to base. He wanted nights with her spent in sheer ecstasy followed by languorous days spent by the water, watching their children play in the surf.

Just the thought of making a family with Lissa sent a trail of goosepimples up his arms and across his shoulders. It all seemed so very real all of a sudden, and an urgency burned in his stomach. He was abundantly clear about what he wanted his life to look like, and he wanted it to start immediately. He picked up his pace, all at once in a rush to get to Lissa, to make things right with her.

If she'd have him.

"Okay. Let's catch up later, then?"

"You got it. Oh, and she's in the private quarters we set up from before you left."

"Thanks, Tomás. For everything."

His brother winked, and then they split off in two separate directions, Tomás tackling the arguably tougher job of filling their father in. That didn't mean the task that lay in front of Gael was easy—not by a long shot. Not to mention the fact that the ramifications of not getting it right were steep.

As he jogged down the entrance hall of the palace toward the guest suites, Gael steeled himself against the idea that Lissa might still decide to turn him away even after he laid his truths and insecurities and shortcomings at her feet. The possibility of losing her was a necessary—albeit scary—risk he was willing to take if it meant they stood a chance at making it past this.

Loving her was a reward he hadn't earned, but he planned to turn that around every day of the rest of his life if she'd let him. They'd overcome so much to get to where they were. Fate had known what she was doing when she plopped them both in the Kelles Islands together, if only they both could get out of their own ways and let her do her damn job.

In a matter of minutes, Gael stood breathless and trembling at the threshold of her suite. The sounds of someone moving around came from behind the door, and his nerves threatened to consume him. In an attempt to summon some much-needed courage, he allowed the future he'd imagined a little bit ago to flash before his eyes.

Kids—their gorgeous children with her hair and sass and their strength—playing on the grounds of his Costa del Sol home.

Lissa in his arms each night, tucked up against his eager frame.

A future that gave her everything her heart desired, starting with the truth.

With that on his mind, he knocked on the door and held his breath until the movement he'd heard earlier made its way to him. He only exhaled when Lissa opened the door and didn't slam it right back in his face. Not that he would have blamed her. He'd been a closed-off, stubborn jerk, and she'd paid the price.

She gestured him inside, but regarded him warily, as if unsure whether he'd come to scold her or sweep her into his arms. She didn't appear to want either. It didn't matter—it was his job to tell her how he felt, then get out of the way and let her decide how to respond.

It sounded easy enough, but the apprehension etched on her face said it wasn't going to be the walk on the beach he'd hoped.

"Hi," he started, not sure where to go from there. His pulse echoed in the cavernous space between his heart and ribcage.

"Hi yourself. Aren't you supposed to be carting me away right about now? I'm shocked I'm not already in cuffs, thrown in the bottom of some dank basement prison for my crimes. Not that anyone has been forthcoming about what those even are—except for the crime of being adopted, which believe me, was as much a surprise to me as it was to you. At least it gave you the get-out-of-jail-free card you wanted, huh? Hell, it gave your family one as well. Now you'll all be rid of me."

Her accusations slashed through him as easily as his officer's sword would have, but he let them penetrate his armor. They were well with her rights to throw at him. Hell, he deserved corporal punishment, so her verbal lashing was a welcome surprise if anything.

"The only crime you're guilty of is loving me. I know you weren't the one who wrote the letter, that it was your father. I think I always knew that but was afraid of what it meant. Still, I'm the villain here, Lissa, and I've come to apologize. I blew it, I know, but I'm here, and I want you to listen."

She smiled, and his heart thumped loud and aggressive against his ribcage, an animal desperate to be freed. Only too late did he recognize the malice tracing her eyes. Malice aimed directly at his overeager heart.

"Oh, you *do*, do you? So, you've realized that keeping secrets about what's happening in my life and who you are, then being closed off to the world no matter how hard those of us who love you try to get in, and—hmmm, I feel like I'm missing something—oh yeah. Then blaming *me* for the threat on my life and treating me like some common two-bit criminal? You realized you were wrong, did you? And after all that—the blame, the wall you built around your heart—you seem to think I should just forgive you for being such a stubborn oaf because you came in and laid it all at my feet?"

She was breathless, as was he, despite being unable to utter a word in his own defense. His eyes were wide, his lips parted in surprise. She was right, plain and simple.

He finally nodded, unable to form any coherent thoughts other than, "Yes. I did. And yes, I hope you will."

Though far too simple of an excuse, those nine words broke through whatever wall she'd put up and her eyes softened around the edges. He exhaled a deep breath that deflated his lungs, carrying out an innate fear she'd send him packing on the warm air. She hadn't told him to shove off, and that was something.

"Good," she tossed back at him, though her voice had lost its aggressive edge. "Continue with that apology, then."

A hint of a smile tugged at the corner of her lips, his cue to lay it all out on the table. All of it. Starting with the little girl in the photo.

"I want to start by telling you about my sister."

Shock registered in the downturn of her brows, the press of her lips. "Your sister?" she replied, her voice tentative. That wasn't what she was expecting, he was sure, but it was the logical place to start. Everything he'd kept hidden, closed off from Lissa was a result of that one paramount, crippling loss.

"The girl in the photo, Michelle. She died of leukemia when I was just a kid, and that's when my parents went off the rails, as you can imagine. The problem was, I never got them back, not really. Not even when Tomás was born a year later. Her loss stayed with our family forever. Honestly, I felt it drowning me on dry land up until the day I met you. You were my breath of fresh air, but it didn't mean she disappeared. Either way, I'm so terribly sorry I didn't share her with you. I felt like I owed my parents the truth about us first before I shared such a tragic part of my history with you, but it was the other way around, actually. I needed to share her with you so that you and I had a future I could share with my family. It took me a little while to see that, but I came around."

She smiled, and it was like sun on his skin, warm and restorative. Something inside him unfroze and liquid hope surged through his veins.

"You did. I can see that. What changed your mind, if

you don't mind me asking?" Her tone had shifted completely, as had her body language. Her arms hung at her sides instead of pulled up tight against her, and her words had all the love and softness as when he'd first seen her at the palace. He wasn't naïve enough to think he was out of the woods yet, but he was making progress, and that was all that counted. He almost tapped out a dance he was so happy, but before he could celebrate, he still had work to do.

"Watching you walk out of that room, I realized I'd messed up. When you granted me a stay of execution, I was so deliriously happy I couldn't wait to share everything with you after we woke up that morning. But, well, you know what happened next."

He filled her in on the parts she didn't know, the information he'd garnered from Tomás. How her father had only recently found out she wasn't his daughter, that this discovery had led to his desperation and the note once he'd realized he couldn't hope to gain any money from her and her marriage if she wasn't of royal lineage. How Lissa's mother had come clean about her brief affair with a man she met at a beachside bar while she vacationed alone when Lissa's father was caught. Lissa had laughed at that part. Then, she'd cried at the loss of her father, the crushing realization that she'd given him all these years and didn't owe him more than a passing glance. She wasn't *his*, which of course she'd told Gael was good news, but also demanded a mourning that he understood. Gael told her she was released from her marital obligation, which had elicited another giggle from Lissa. She'd sobered when Gael continued to inform her about his conversation with Tomás, and what fruits that had provided for them both. After he was done, she'd shuddered and shaken her head in seeming disbelief, then dried her tears on her sleeve, a weak smile on her lips.

"I wish I'd never answered that damned phone call, Liss," he said, his voice solemn and quiet.

She moved close enough for him to touch, and the temptation to close the millimeters between them almost consumed him. But he knew if he laid a finger on that delectable, smooth skin of hers, he'd whisk her to the bedroom and they'd be right back where they started. They worked when it came to physical intimacy, but they needed to work on the rest. So, he shoved ideas of her naked form against his down with his libido and concentrated on her eyes instead.

They'd filled with moisture again, and a few errant tears spilled over onto her cheeks. Damn. His plan to keep his distance from her backfired, and he rubbed the pad of his thumb across her jawline. As his skin touched hers, a tremor coursed through them both, so fierce he wasn't sure whose body it originated in.

"You had to," she whispered, seemingly as affected as he was by the electric charge still pulsing between them. "It's just what came after that I could have done without. How could you believe…"

He cut her off with a kiss, his lips pressing down gently on hers at first until her arms wrapped around his neck, her fingers tangled in his hair. Then he was two years younger, kissing a fiery woman he'd met at the beachside bar again for the first time. He recalled the way her taste swam inside his mouth, infiltrating his senses, rendering him just as dumb as he was now. She'd branded him then, made him her own in that single moment. He'd fallen more in love with her every moment since, but it had all started then, with that first kiss.

In so many ways, they were the same youthful kids they were back then. God knew she tasted the same, felt the same as the day he'd met her. Since that day, however, they'd been through so much, changed in tiny, imperceptible ways that left them strangers to each other.

That was why this kiss was their new beginning. He would continue to fall more in love with Lissa every day he was lucky enough to have her in his arms like this. She opened her mouth and deepened the kiss, and then he forgot every negative experience of his life. When her tongue teased his out and tangled with it, he let go of the pain of forsaking his birthright, the agony of losing his little sister, the damage his parents piled on top of all of them after her death. There was only Lissa and their future.

He pulled back and smiled, his eyes now as damp as hers.

"I didn't. Not really. Will you let me make it up to you? Every day as long as both of us are alive?"

She smiled—the same smile she'd worn on the night he'd met her gaze over a beer and martini and come out of it a changed man, a better man. His chest warmed with the unspoken affection he hadn't yet earned but accepted nonetheless.

"Before I answer that, I have a question of my own, Capítan."

"I'll answer anything you ask from this day until our last, Lissa, *mi amor.*"

"Knowing what you do now, about my crazy family and the drama that seems bent on following us wherever we are, do you really still love me?"

"Oh, Liss," he growled, finally pulling her as tight into his chest as he could without crushing the air from her chest. "I love you more today than I did making love to you by the Cantabrian Sea. More than lying beside you in the Pyrenees. I love you so much I think I might be a terminal case. Can you handle that?"

She pushed up on her toes and crushed her lips to his, claiming him as hers in the way they both knew best. They'd learn other ways in time, but for now, loving her like this and being loved in return, was all Gael had ever hoped for or would again.

"Yes," she breathed. "I can handle that." And she kissed him again, their future as certain and passion-filled as any had ever been.

EPILOGUE: TWO YEARS LATER

"I know where we are, *amor*. Is this blindfold really necessary?" Gael asked.

Lissa frowned, even though she wasn't remotely upset and Gael couldn't see the change in her expression either way.

"How did you know?" she goaded him.

"You think I could honestly ever forget the scent of this ocean, this body of water where I first kissed you, first touched you—"

She coughed, cutting him off before he kept going down that line of conversation. What he couldn't see from behind his blindfold would certainly get them both in trouble if he shared out loud what they'd actually done in that body of water.

"Okay, fine. I'll take it off. But that doesn't mean the surprise is over."

"Whatever you say, Mrs. Reyes. Just so long as you know I don't need surprises to stay madly in love with you. Our life together is all I could ever want or need…" He trailed off as she removed the blindfold and watched with a smug satisfaction as his eyes adjusted to the light on the southernmost beach on the Kelles Islands. When they'd been there last, they'd been trapped by a storm that had ravaged the island, but now, the sun was out and not a cloud dotted the perfect horizon.

"What the—" he asked, and Lissa laughed out loud, a full-fledged guffaw that had only begun since the night Gael had come to her room and told her everything about his—and her—life. The night they'd started over both as people and as a couple. So much had changed since then, from their engagement, to their elopement, and his command of the Royal Naval Fleet. Little did he know the change that had already begun inside her that was sure to upend both their worlds. In the best way, of course.

"Thank God. I was getting tired of listening to you yammer on about how great this girl is. I was beginning to think you knew I was here the whole time and you were rubbing it in since I was engaged to her first." Tomás laughed and slapped his brother on the shoulder.

Lissa's chest warmed and expanded with a sense of belonging and love she hadn't ever felt before. The two years without Gael after meeting him and falling in love with him in these very islands were the toughest she'd ever endured. But now, witnessing the family their love had built there to support them, it was all worth it.

"What the heck are you doing on my anniversary trip?" Gael asked, but Lissa saw the smile tugging on his lips. He was as happy as she was they were all there.

"Dani and I couldn't let you come here alone again, could we? You two got in a helluva lot of trouble last time you were left unattended in the Islands."

Gael laughed then and pulled Lissa close. He kissed her on the top of the head and her stomach flipped as it always did when he was this close to her. Would she ever grow used to him, or worse yet, bored of him? She didn't think so. Not ever.

"Well, what trouble could we possibly get in? We're already hitched. All that's left to do is start a family…" he said, gazing down at her with love and a lust she could see brimming.

Tomás opened his mouth to speak, but Lissa waved him off.

"I've got this one, *hermanito*," she said, using the nickname she'd adopted for Tomás. He'd always been like a little brother to her, and now it was official. Although, soon—eight months to be exact—she'd have to get used to calling him *tio*. "Love," she said, meeting her husband's heated gaze, "I think we've already taken care of that last part, too."

He turned her around so she faced him, and she searched his eyes for disappointment or hurt—after all they hadn't planned on adding to their family so soon. That was what their trip to the Kelles was originally designed for. When she'd discovered the delightful surprise of her slightly early pregnancy, she'd roped Tomás and his new love, Dani, into joining them to celebrate the new life and addition to the Reyes family.

She didn't find a single reticent feature on his perfect, handsome face. All she saw as she gazed into her husband's crystal-blue eyes was love. And that was all she'd ever needed.

He bent down to kiss her and just like that, another kiss led to another new beginning for them both.

CHECK OUT THE FIRST BOOK IN AN ALDONIA ROYALS SERIES: *AN HEIR FOR THE SECRET PRINCE*

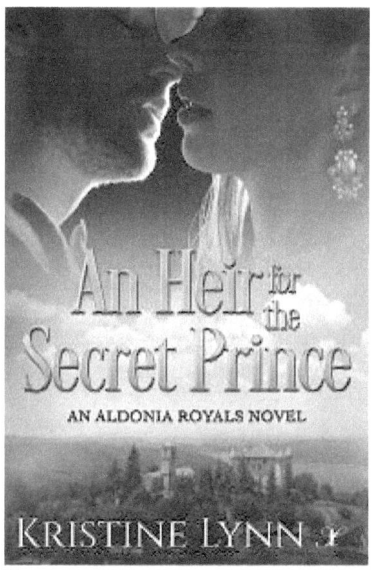

Okay, who invited the journalist?

Philip, advisor to the Prince of Aldonia, is livid when he discovers someone invited a nosy reporter to the palace to write a salacious story about the royal family. The problem is, the more she digs into their pasts, the more she will find out about him—and his private life is none of her damn business. Which is why no one is more shocked than him when, on a whim, he asks her to stay on as his guest.

Aurelia is only certain of two things when she meets Philip on assignment in Aldonia: he's hot as melted sin on a cracker and he's hiding something. Too bad he's NOT the story she's there for. However, that won't stop her from finding out just why he's so reclusive—and tempting.

However, when their growing attraction takes an unexpected turn, Philip may be forced to share his darkest secrets with Aurelia—secrets that will change her life. Will their new relationship be strong enough to overcome the adversity these revelations bring?

EXCERPT:

The truth was, Aurelia didn't care in the least about Prince Gregory or his fortune. He was a story, plain and simple. A means to an end that came with a week abroad on assignment in a place that served dang good wine and hors "oeuvres.

When one of the women cackled, a high-pitched sound not unlike the hyenas from The Lion King, Aurelia let the giggle escape. It was louder than the noise from the idle conversations, and a few heads turned to look at her.

"Ms. Beck?"

Aurelia choked on her wine as she spun around to face the owner of the deep, sexy voice behind her, sloshing a good deal of what was left in her glass on his shoes in the process. Her heels caught on the long hem of her dress and she nearly toppled over.

Instead, strong hands wrapped around her, locking her in place. Her hand not holding the crystal stemware was pressed against a solid wall of muscled flesh, steadying herself.

"Crap," she muttered, looking down at the shiny black loafers that now had a third of her Merlot on them, patting the chest of the man who'd saved her from eating concrete. "I'm terribly sorry. I was waiting to speak with," she started, her arm flailing behind her in an errant attempt to point out the Prince, but her words—usually her specialty—stuck in her throat.

There, in front of her, his hands still gripping her bare arms, was the most breathtakingly beautiful man she'd ever seen.

Goosebumps erupted over her skin and heat flushed her cheeks.

Good God above.

CHECK OUT THE SECOND BOOK IN AN ALDONIA ROYALS SERIES: *A BRIDE FOR THE ALDONIAN KING*

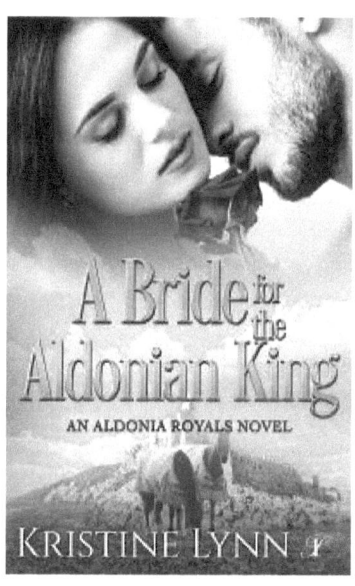

Lorelai is back home to take over her late father's management of the royal stables. Heartbroken over the loss of her father and determined to become the first female Royal Huntswoman, the last thing she needs is to run into the subject of her schoolgirl fantasies—the current King of Aldonia. When Lorelai is forced to work with King Robert, she discovers two facts that may just reignite her old flame for him: he's a terrific single father, and he's not the spoiled, rich brat she remembers from her youth.

King Robert knows his past didn't paint him in a good light—he was spoiled, stubborn, and a lothario who took no prisoners where love was concerned. But he's changed—the horrific loss of his parents and a messy divorce made sure of that. So, when a mysterious new hire for his royal stables shows up with a grudge for injustices he can't recall, he is determined to make things right with her. On the way to winning her over, though, he finds himself falling head over heels in love, despite making a solemn promise to himself to never go down that road again.

Will they find their way through their separate hurts to allow themselves a second chance at love? Or is too late?

Discover the breathtaking country of Aldonia as you root for Robert and Lorelai's love story! For more of the Aldonian royal world (and the first installment of the Aldonia Royals series), check out An Heir for the Secret Prince.

EXCERPT:

As the owner of the voice rounded the corner, Lorelai's breath halted in her chest. It wasn't only the voice that was sexier, stronger, more masculine. Heck if the past ten years hadn't done Robert, Duke of Puruse, King of Aldonia, a world of good. Wide hands sat atop hips that boasted snug jeans that left little to the imagination.

He squinted, but even in the dull light of the stable, Lorelai saw that his eyes were the same pale blue—maybe the only part of him that was remotely the same. Only the edges showed wear in the thin, almost invisible lines that flanked each eye. Darn men for only getting more good-looking with age. As if she needed another reason to despise him.

He walked toward her and Ginny, rubbing his eyes. Lorelai tried not to stare at the way the striated muscles in his arms pulsed with this simple gesture. He was all muscle, hard edges now. *Christ.*

When she'd known him as a teen, he'd been pudgy, adorable in his know-it-all-ness, but certainly not what one would describe as naturally handsome. Now, though, he could be the model for older men who found the gym late in life, leading to a total transformation.

Oh, goody.

He wasn't only back—the how and why still escaped her for now—but looked better than ever. She had a few choice words brewing for her brother, who hadn't given her so much as a warning. So much for a smooth takeover of the barn and operation. Lorelai's mind was now firmly set on one thing, and one thing only.

She would become the huntsman and make him rue the day he treated her like a child.

AVAILABLE WHERE ALL BOOKS ARE SOLD. BUY A COPY FOR YOURSELF!

ACKNOWLEDGEMENTS

I'd like to thank so many people for the production of this book. Melissa, my publisher, for starters. Inkspell has been a joy to work with and I love being part of this family. I'd also like to thank Audrey, my editor extraordinaire. As supporters go, I'd like to start with the two best writing partners a gal could ask for. Anna and Kate, I wouldn't be here without you two. Our phone calls are the wind beneath my wings, the butter to my toast, the oil to The Rock's abs. Thanks for being amazing friends and champions of my work.

Same goes for Erica and Stacy. You both have been there from the start and I'm eternally grateful for your friendship.

To my daughter, Iz—all I hope is that you keep writing your stories (and finish one!) so I can read about how great a mom I was in your acknowledgement section. On a serious note, though, I love you to the end of the earth and back. Thanks for being my OG writing partner, typing away at your novels while I stressed over mine. You're the best friend-daughter-colleague I dreamed about.

Finally, to my parents. You two are my first beta readers and biggest supporters. Even though I know you secretly wish I wrote true crime or murder documentaries, I'm grateful for your help and loving support. (And the use of the Mexico place as a writing retreat. You can't take it back—it's in print.)

ABOUT THE AUTHOR

Kristine Lynn is the author of the *Treasure Valley* and *Secret Prince* romance series, as well as the linked collection of short stories, *Shrapnel*. When she's not writing, she's teaching college students in Arizona and enjoying the Southwest with her daughter, puppy, and three-quarters of a desert tortoise. To connect with Kristine (who also writes under Kama O'Connor), you can email her at kristinelynnauthor@gmail.com or follow her on social media.

Twitter: @kristinelauthor
Facebook: @kristinelynnauthor
Goodreads:
https://www.goodreads.com/user/show/19811168-kama-o-connor
Website:
https://kristinelynn.wixsite.com/author/about